GRAY SKIES

Elle Emtage

GRAY SKIES

iUniverse books may be ordered through booksellers or by contacting:

iUniverse
1663 Liberty Drive
Bloomington, IN 47403
www.iuniverse.com
1-800-Authors (1-800-288-4677)

ISBN: 978-1-4917-3086-7 (sc)
ISBN: 978-1-4917-3087-4 (hc)
ISBN: 978-1-4917-3088-1 (e)

Library of Congress Control Number: 2014908098

Printed in the United States of America.

iUniverse rev. date: 06/23/2014

Chapter 1

———⌇⋅⌇⋅⌇⋅⌇⋅⌇———

I shivered lightly and looked outside. We were in the middle of autumn, and chilly air greeted the curling smoke of the engine's exhaust. The folder beside me was filled with invoices, receipts, schedules, and other documents. I took it up and studied the features of the young CEO emblazoned on the cover who seemed to glare right back at me. We had been on the train for the last seven weeks, prepping each stop for the arrival of his train, which was traveling two weeks behind us. I returned the folder beside me and snuggled into the down comforter and fell asleep almost immediately. Weird as it might seem, I actually liked sleeping on the train. For as long as I could remember, it felt as though I wasn't getting enough sleep. My dreams were interlaced with people and places I didn't know. In the last few weeks I'd begun having nightmares that all ended the same way—with me falling into a never-ending pool of white light. Often, the whole experience left me with a pounding headache when I awoke.

The hum of the train, however, lulled me to peaceful sleep on most occasions. On this occasion, the change of speed when the train came to a halt roused me from my dream of billowing clouds and dancing shadows. I quickly put on my jacket and steadied myself. I looked outside and was awed by the sight. We had arrived in Italy just after the summer tourist rush. It was the only place

I knew that got greener as winter approached. I was pleasantly surprised by the lush landscape dotted with wild boars, hares, and pheasants, which I was sure were embracing the freedom of a tourist-free landscape. I briefly caught sight of worn cobblestone paths and structures which seemed to be lost in time, and in a few moments I felt an unexplained peace wash over me.

Around eight weeks ago, I had packed my bags, left Japan, and joined in on the bright idea of our public relations department: a ten-week stint aboard a train as a good way for the owner of the company to build relationships and foster employee relations. Because he employed just over thirty thousand, very few ever met Dunstan Moab in person. He shied away from the public eye, and his private life was very private. On the rare occasion that he was actually seen outside his corporate office, he seemed to be continuously shrouded in lawyers and administrative assistants.

I disembarked and picked up the nervous energy from my colleagues almost instantly. On the stop before this one, we had learned that he had joined my train, thus missing three stops. It was a logistics nightmare, but I had to admit that even I was a little giddy when I found out that he was on the same train, a giddiness that intensified when I caught a glimpse of him in the dining cabin once or twice. He was just as astonishingly good-looking in person as he was in every other medium that I had seen him in, dispelling any notions of falsity created by airbrushing.

Dunstan stood just over six feet with dark wavy hair. His eyebrows were perfectly arched over ash gray eyes, but there was a veil of sadness in the creases of his brow. His olive-hued skin was impossibly smooth. I surmised that this was a result of lavish massages, luxurious spa days, and a very balanced and catered diet. To me he seemed impossibly perfectly proportioned, and I couldn't stop looking at his face. If he wasn't a multimillionaire mega mogul, he easily could have been a poster boy for some obscure brand of jeans, designer cologne, or excessively expensive underwear.

We all bustled over to a temporary meeting room that had been converted for the operations team. I was in awe of the brand-new station, which was a close replica of the Riyadh metro station, right down its reflective canopies, steel and glass facades, and tree-lined central atrium. I found a quiet spot near one of the bars, away from the bustling operations team, to organize the rest of my day. In a few minutes I noticed raised voices of people around me and peeped around the beautifully potted plant to see what was happening. There he was, scanning the buzzing entourage of employees that fluttered around him, listening carefully with his head slightly tilted as he was briefed on his schedule. I didn't think that he had any idea what his early visit had done to create total panic and chaos in my camp.

I moved to the executive lounge, one of fifteen that had been built at selected station stops, to meet with the chef of the restaurant that Mr. Moab would be visiting that night. I spoke quickly to the nervous chef in his native tongue instead of English, to get through the conversation quickly and more easily. I calmed him as best as I could and upon conclusion went on to take an incoming call from the Japanese office. They were stressing about the collapse of one of the real estate deals we'd left for them to seal. I ducked behind one of the larger pillars closer to the bar so that I could speak firmly yet kindly to the frantic Japanese. A bartender near me watched somewhat curiously with a boyish smile on his lips. People were sometimes curious about how quickly I could switch languages, though to me it was just natural. Or maybe he was working up the nerve to ask me something. He looked me over appreciatively and nodded toward the glasses of breakfast drinks waiting, to which I shook my head.

Like I could afford to drink right now, I thought, although a stiff shot of something bitter and potent might do me good right about now. I turned to face the bartender as I listened to the issues on the other line and became so absorbed in my conversation that I barely glimpsed his sudden change in stature as he looked over my shoulder at someone behind me. I whirled around and crashed into muscle and bone beneath taut skin and a wonderfully sweet but subtle musk.

"I'm so sorry," I muttered. I looked up, and my heart came to a complete stop when I realized I had accidentally bumped into Dunstan himself.

"It's okay," he replied, his hand reaching out to steady me as I almost lost my balance. Somehow his voice matched his appearance. "Dunstan Moab," he said with an outstretched hand. As I returned the gesture, I hoped that my palms weren't sweaty. For a fleeting moment I could have sworn that his grasp was shaky, but surely that was my imagination.

"Yes, yes, I know who you are." Those were the only words I could muster at first. "My name is Destiny Tallum—I'm attached to Language and Logistics," I said after a pause, sounding much more confident than I felt.

"Ah, yes, the language expert," he said more casually than I'd expected. "I've heard good things about you and your team. Keep up the great work."

He ordered his drink, and I swallowed the lump in my throat. Thank God that my jacket hid the traces of perspiration threatening to stain the silk of my inner blouse just from the sound of his voice. It was commanding yet gentle and polite. He could make you want to do what he asked without being forceful. I took a sharp breath to counter the light-headedness that I felt. Apparently, I had forgotten to breathe. He had the scent of masculinity—that was the only way I could describe it. It was woodsy, mixed with a sprinkling of fresh linen. His lips parted slightly to reveal perfectly framed teeth, which seemed natural but impossibly white. A vein throbbed slightly in his defined neck, and as he swallowed, I noticed that it moved with the act. It was cute. His nose was perfectly proportioned, and his eyebrows looked as though they were etched in place. It was impossible for one being to be so perfectly made. His body was taut and lean, and although I could probably spend a night or two dreaming about what he looked like beneath the layers of clothing, it was his eyes that held me captive.

"How are you coping on this trip?" He asked. I mustered enough self-control to provide him with a response.

"Everything is going according to plan." I was vaguely aware that despite my efforts to appear calm and collected, my heart was doing flip flops all over itself, and I was praying that he did not notice. Beneath striking long eyelashes lay pools of gray light shimmering in the morning sun. I felt lost in his eyes. There were no words to describe them. His eyes appeared almost transparent, yet they seemed to bore right through to my soul. His dark eyebrows arched perfectly away from his eyes, as if he wanted to know more about everything.

"It's different, but in a good way." I added. He simply nodded and turned his head back to the bartender, who served him, and, to my surprise Dunstan politely thanked him and dropped a tip in the tip jar before walking away, briefly stopping to nod to me as he turned. Within a few moments he was enveloped in his crowd of people, and I was left fanning the flames that leaped around my heart.

I finished the series of meetings that I had set for the day long after Dunstan had left the lounge, but I couldn't get his face out of my mind. My head throbbed dully as I recounted the thirty-second encounter. How was it that impossibly rich people could also be so impossibly breathtaking? I had followed his movements throughout the evening and carefully observed his interactions with everyone he came into contact with. At moments, I worried he might think I was stalking him—well, to be truthful, I was—but I was sure that I'd camouflaged my efforts to the best of my ability.

Before meeting him, I had told myself that he was probably arrogant and self-centered, knowing that all these people were at his beck and call, yet his voice was surprisingly gentle, and he was pointedly polite as I watched him during one of his briefings during the day. He listened attentively when spoken to, although I could almost see the mechanisms in his mind whirring away in between conversations. His gray eyes would darken in concentration and become light in laughter. Surprisingly he did that too—laugh. I didn't know what I expected of him, so I pocketed the memory of the day and headed back to the train to wrap things up with my team.

A few days later, we approached our next stop, the city of Milan. I was looking forward to that visit because it had been some time since I had been in the city. I had a few hours free in the morning, so I wandered the streets to the Civic Gallery of Modern Art. I spent an hour walking through the museum, enthralled by the pieces on display and admiring the great collections of paintings, mainly by Italians of the nineteenth century. But what I loved even more was the villa itself and the magnificent garden behind it. I absolutely adored this tiny bit of paradise in the buzzing city. A small falls with a pond was home to ducks and swans, and just being there made you feel rested. It was unseasonably warm, and there were several locals and tourists taking advantage of the huge lawn. Despite the beautiful surroundings I was blessed with, I couldn't ignore the pang of loneliness I felt as I watched families huddling together while pointing at the city's sights.

In the gardens I noticed two guys in animated conversation and found myself drawn to them. One of them held the hand of a bouncy blonde who seemed only partially interested in their conversation. She turned around, and for a brief moment, when our eyes met, I was certain that she smiled at me. I politely returned the gesture and found myself wandering toward them. However, before I got any farther than a few steps, another group joined them, and they headed away from me. They all seemed vaguely familiar, but they were too far away for me to figure out who they were. I continued walking with no real direction, and I could see them in the distance still engrossed in their conversations. Pretty soon the blonde who had smiled at me planted a long kiss on the lips of the one holding her hand, and I could feel a tug on my heart strings. This was met with some sort of playful banter directed to the one who had received the affection of the blonde. She turned around suddenly and looked in my direction once again before entering the building, and I was sure that she smiled at me once more.

The other group members now stopped and appeared to resume their conversation. I was drawn to them and couldn't seem to stop staring at them. At one point one of the taller guys looked in my direction, even pausing long enough to shade his eyes against the sun. I wasn't sure who or what he was looking at, and I couldn't make out his features beneath the hat that was pulled low, almost covering his eyes. I quickly turned my head, and by the time I glanced back again, the group was gone. *Why did I do that?* I wondered. I just couldn't seem to open up to anyone at all. As silly as I knew it would sound to others, I felt as though I belonged to someone, and fate just hadn't drawn us together yet. *I would like to belong to young Mr. Dunstan though!* I thought. I giggled and walked back into the gallery.

I headed back to the Dream Scape office and sat at one of the hot desks designated for those of us who popped into the branch from time to time. I decided that I would catch up with my e-mails and then check in with the office in Japan to tie up any loose ends. My boss came by and summoned the small team together. She stood above most of us and exuded confidence as she spoke. Not much older than I, she was a stunning 5'10" with unbelievably long legs and a smile that could light up an arena. You felt like you were in the shadows when you stood next to her. She simply drew people to her like a magnet, and whether you liked her or not, you did as she asked, sometimes without even realizing it. Slightly melodramatic, she was also a passionate professional totally dedicated to her job.

Vera McMaster headed the Eastern and Pacific liaison office for Dream Scape Inc. She was tough as nails, intelligent, and beautiful. She worked hard and played harder. She was ruthless yet fair, and she demanded 100 percent from us on good days and 150 percent on bad ones. She hailed from California and had that blonde bombshell look about her. She used all of her gifts and talents to get where she wanted to be. She loved traveling and seemed thrilled at a challenge, and often took on tasks that were too daunting for the other heads. She was very selective in her choice of staff, so there was no doubt we were handpicked by her to be part of her team.

Less than half an hour later, as we were finishing, the office administrator summoned Vera over. With Italian heritage, Vera spoke to the administrator in mediocre Italian as she excitedly conveyed a message. Vera was almost glowing when she turned back to us and said, "That's a wrap, guys. I have a lunch meeting with Mr. Moab, so we will speak again tomorrow."

It seemed she'd forgotten my linguistic skills—because the message given to her was an invitation for her entire senior team. I was miffed at being excluded from another opportunity to be around Dunstan Moab, but I said nothing to the others because I knew that her actions would cause discord, and right now we needed to work as a team. I smiled inwardly as she practically skipped out of the room. It was no secret that Vera had a thing for Dunstan, and although the rest of us had never met him personally—except for my brief encounter the day before—she often dropped comments about fabulous events and outings she attended "on our behalf." She was enraptured by him, and if you listened to the office buzz, according to her, Dunstan never shrugged off her advances either. I turned my attention back to my mail and was done within the hour, at which point I headed off to the cafeteria for a midmorning mocha fix. Pretty soon the rest of the team joined me.

There were twelve junior assistants, and of these the five seniors were Roth, Ethan, Anna, Stella, and me. I was the youngest on the team, and many times it felt as though I had to work twice as hard to prove my worth. Roth was burly and built, whereas Ethan was agile and shrewd-looking. Stella had a timeless beauty about her. She had long, dark hair, and her European accent made her seem exotic. She was always pleasant and professional in all of our interactions, but she seemed guarded with everyone, like she was carrying some deep, dark secret that could be revealed if anyone got too close. She was the complete opposite of her husband Ethan, and it was with him I was closest. He was super-protective of me, and I found that he was good company. Roth and Anna were an item, both in their early thirties, and seemed to be perfectly compatible in every way. Their pairings made sense since we were never anywhere long enough to meet anyone new.

Ethan had taken me under his wing practically from the first day that I joined the operations team, which now caused some tension between me and Stella, but really, she had nothing to worry about. Ethan was the closest and maybe the only real friend I had that I could share anything with. He was like a favorite uncle and always seemed to be keeping an eye out for me. This rustled Stella's feathers; she seemed to feel threatened by our closeness. Eventually

I had given up trying to assure her that I was solely focused on advancing my career with the company.

Dream Scape Inc. managed every form of talent imaginable, from the music industry to corporate portfolios and sports—it even owned a few teams. It represented many authors, actors, writers, and dancers. If someone did it well, Dream Scape Inc. managed it. Several celebrities had even dropped their current agents and managers in a bid to acquire management from the company. The firm enlisted lawyers, financiers, and administrative departments and opened offices in every place that major talent resided—which meant we had offices globally. The company used social networks to find talent and employed four hundred or so persons just to stay online all day to surf for talent. Dream Scape even found talent to manage the talent, and most if not all of the employees had been actively recruited by the firm.

Among us we had a staff of fifty, and we worked closely with our sourcing team. The latter had recruited close to three thousand talents—as we called them—from several hundred thousand applicants in less than six months. This meant Legal had been pulling overtime shifts sorting contracts, while Dream Agents pushed to find them work, and all of the supporting staff then had to pull extra hours supporting them in addition to the other offices around the world. This time around, we were all very tired from the Japanese expansion.

We immediate team members considered ourselves to be a close-knit family of sorts, and whenever we had the chance, we explored whatever country we happened to have a break in. We celebrated the holidays together and spent vacations away. Our work and social lives seemed wonderfully meshed, and even though I was the odd unpaired woman, that didn't bother me so much that I didn't join them every once in a while. I was a bit of a people-watcher and could just as easily quietly observe as interact. On our first night in Milan, we planned for a night on the town and caught the sights and sounds of the old and the new. I was in love with the country and decided that perhaps I would figure out a way to set up shop in Italy for good.

The next day, we were still buzzing from the wonderful art and history we had seen from the night before, and although the rest of the group planned to attend a popular fashion event later that evening, after a relatively long day at work, I felt like having a night out alone, exploring the city scene and people-watching on my own. I liked to imagine where they were from, what were they going home to at the end of the evening, and what perhaps greeted them in the morning. After a late-evening stroll, I found a charming restaurant with outdoor seating. I sat partially facing the restaurant but with still enough of an outside view that I could watch the locals and tourists pass by. I placed my order and sat back in the chair and looked around. As I glanced inside, to my surprise there was Dunstan Moab, sitting on his own and just placing his order as well. He looked up at that very moment, and our eyes met. He lifted his glass in a toast and simply nodded and smiled. I hoped that he didn't think I was stalking him, but it was strange that we'd ended up in the same restaurant.

I tried not to look back at him but kept finding my eyes wandering in his direction. He was wearing a black sweater that fitted him well. The combination of the sweater and his dark hair and coloring made him look dark and mysterious, and he stood out among the diners. I still couldn't get over how attractive he was. As my meal was being served, I heard the all-too-familiar voice of Vera as she rounded the corner. She was on the phone issuing an instruction and letting the person on the other end know that she was meeting Dunstan for dinner which he had requested at the last minute. She smiled when she saw me, but said nothing as she waltzed by to join him. I saw him stand and hold her chair for her and then offer to take her coat. She reached over and kissed him on both cheeks and whispered something in his ear; he laughed. Beneath her coat, she wore a beautiful peach blouse that amplified her cleavage more than necessary. From the looks of their interaction, I figured this wasn't a work meeting, and suddenly my appetite waned. Nevertheless, I had already ordered, and recognizing that my jealousy made no sense at all, I adjusted my chair so that my back was to the restaurant and tried to ignore the couple inside.

Occasionally, I could hear Vera's laugh above the clatter and chatter of the restaurant, and although I didn't hear Dunstan at any point, I assumed that he was the one making her so thoroughly enjoy herself. I sat there long after my meal was complete, sipping a cappuccino and just watching the passersby. I didn't hear or see Dunstan and Vera standing over me until Vera called my name.

"Destiny," she said, and I could tell from the irritation in her voice that this was the second or third time she'd called my name. "Destiny," she repeated.

I looked up and set my cup on the table. I noticed that Vera had her hand neatly tucked in Dunstan's arm, and I had to admit that they made a cute couple. Her fairness and his darkness complemented each other well.

"Good evening, Vera. Mr. Moab," I said, standing to shake Dunstan's hand.

"You're out pretty late on your own," Vera said, almost swatting my hand away.

I pretended that I didn't notice her gesture and held back my own slap, which I imagined delivering to her face. "Just having a quick dinner and some downtime," I replied.

"Well, you be careful heading back to the train tonight on your own," Vera said absently, more to the air than to me; her eyes never really left Dunstan. If I wasn't mistaken, Dunstan looked pensive and tired, but he merely nodded.

I nodded too and assured her that I would be cautious. I then watched them walk down the cobbled pathway, arm in arm, without Dunstan saying a word to me. *Whatever*, I thought and continued my people-watching. Now irritated and agitated, I decided to leave and asked for my bill the next time my waiter came by.

"Signorina," the waiter said, a confused expression on his face, "the bill, it has been taken care of by il signore, your friend who just left."

I thanked him and tried to leave him a tip, which he also refused, saying that it had been taken care of too. I shook my head and headed back to the station, irritated with myself that I felt as though my evening had been ruined, without just cause. I was also confused as to why Mr. Moab would pay for my dinner. Was this some sort of patronizing gesture on his part? Did he think that I would have dinner at a restaurant that I couldn't afford? I wanted to stay mad, but I couldn't because deep down I felt that it really had been just a kind gesture on his part, though surmising something more sinister felt better in light of seeing him and Vera together.

Chapter 2

—⁓ⲟⲟⲉⲣⲟⲟⲕⲉⲟⲟⲱ—

The following day, at just after ten in the evening, our team was operating at full speed as we finished the final preparations for the spectacular program that the company would be presenting to its employees, its clients, and the press the next day. The series of meetings would end with a concert featuring several popular American and European artists as a joint humanitarian effort for various Dream Scape charities. I had remained quiet throughout the day, as Vera had ensured that everyone in her circle—which meant the entire team—knew about yet another dinner with Dunstan. I told no one that he had paid for my dinner since I was still unsure as to why he had. I felt irritated and twitchy and decided that I needed some fresh air. Milan, though beautiful in all its city glamour, sometimes felt overwhelming. It was rare to find any vegetation in the city, so the wooded area just outside the event spot was just what I needed.

After a few minutes, I heard a soft yet urgent wailing; I thought it sounded like a child. I wandered toward the sound, knowing a child shouldn't be outside at this time of night. As I drew closer to the wooded area outside of the parking lot, I realized that the sound I was hearing was actually that of a kitten. Somewhere outside in the chilly night air, there was a stranded animal, and my heart ached for it. I looked back at the concert hall and noted that there were a few people still lingering and made a judgment call about whether to venture into the wooded area on my own. It couldn't be far, I thought, and I couldn't help it—I was a cat person. Just a few feet in, I stopped and called, "Here, kitty! Where are you?" I was hoping against all hope that it was nearby. Thankfully, I looked up, and there it was—seemingly stuck in a tree. "Here, kitty. How did you get all the way up there? Come on down." I tried coaxing it, but it just stared at me with doleful eyes, trembling with each meow. I realized now that it was terrified, and I feared the animal would try to jump and break its neck. I looked around for some help, but the others were too far away. I had no other choice but to try a rescue operation and hope that there wouldn't be two victims calling for help shortly.

After a few more minutes of futile coaxing, I threw my hands in the air. "You aren't going to make me come up there, are you?"

The kitten remained quiet and still, its bright eyes now wide with intrigue.

"Okay, kitty, I'm coming up." I wasn't exactly athletic, but I wasn't unfit either, so it didn't look like too daunting a task. I made my way carefully up the tree, while trying to quietly convince the kitten not to move. It alternated between backing away and advancing as I got nearer, but I needed it to come toward me more because I could see that the branch the kitten was precariously perched on was too weak to support my weight. When I got as far as my weight on the branch would allow, the kitten froze.

No amount of coaxing would budge it, and it stared at me with big beautiful eyes, the wind rustling through its fur. At a lower height, I would have considered lunging for it and hoping for a soft fall, but I was at least ten feet in the air, and the ground below was riddled with roots and pointy branches.

"Come on, kitty," I whined. "I came all this way for you—you've got to work with me now." The small creature seemed to be trying to make up its mind when a slight gust of cold air made the decision. The kitten sniffed the air and arched its back as if it had picked up a new scent. As it stood still with bright eyes looking beyond me in the direction of the wind, I had the opportunity to take a closer look at this light gray kitten with bright blue eyes. It had long whiskers and almost a slight pout with pink lips. Its fur looked healthy, but it was so tiny and wet that its fur stuck to its skin, making it look even smaller. I was sure that the kitten could fit in the palm of my hand. My heart melted; I had to coax it down. I lay flat on the branch and tested my weight on it. It held, so I began crawling forward slowly on my belly. It started tentatively toward me, meowing softly as if asking me to stay still, as if to say that it was coming.

Just as the kitten got close enough for me to reach for it, it froze and backed away and then froze again. After a few seconds, the kitten became alert and looked beyond me. It sniffed the air, and its eyes became wide again as the kitten looked deeper into the woods.

"Great," I muttered. *Now I am going to be mauled by some night creature while trying to rescue a schizophrenic kitten.*

Then it occurred to me that there were worse things out there, and I was out here to face them alone. Although the area was relatively well lit from the lights in the parking lot, there were dark spots in the woods that extended beyond the reach of the lights. And of course, no one knew where I was. So I did like the feline and froze. It was then that I heard a light rustling on the path—like running feet. As I heard the steps coming closer, I held my breath and prayed that what or who it was wouldn't smell me or look up. My beautiful kitten decided at that exact moment to meow once again. The steps stopped directly beneath us.

Hey," a voice said in the shadows, "what are you doing up there?" Before I could answer, the subject of my rescue mission jumped over me, scampered down the tree with ease, and landed clumsily at the feet of the voice, meowing all the way. The gentle rage that threatened to make me hurry down the tree behind it subsided as I felt the branch bend slightly beneath me.

I was in a quandary: I couldn't stay in the tree, yet I wasn't sure who was down there because I was facing the wrong direction. It finally dawned on me that this had not been a good idea, and to my dismay I too was stuck now. I needed to turn around somehow, but without knowing who I would be backing into, I paused to give myself time to decide what to do.

As if understanding my predicament, the person below spoke up again. "Listen, you can't stay up there. Are you okay? Do you need help to get down?" Suddenly, the voice became plainly familiar. Embarrassment washed over me as I realized the identity of the runner who had a firsthand view of my butt.

"No," I almost groaned, "I've got it, Mr. Moab." I tried to back down, but I heard the branch crack and split, so I froze once again and prepared for the inevitable. In a few seconds, the branch gave way, and gravity pulled me toward the ground, though my pride kept my scream stifled in my lungs. Luckily, there was another branch a few feet below, and somehow the two branches became intertwined. I was clutching the branch with my eyes closed tight, again bracing myself for the fall, when I felt strong arms grab me around the waist.

"Now I've got you," Dunstan said as I slid down his body to land somewhat ungracefully at his feet.

"Thanks." Although I was embarrassed, my heart still pounded in excitement as he cupped my chin and pulled my face up.

"Are you okay?" he asked softly. "Are you hurt?" His fingers seemed to sting my face, and my pulse sped dangerously past normal levels. I felt giddy and tried to steady my weakening knees, but my feet were caught in the vines. I fell forward into him, and we both landed in the soft shrub behind him. Lying awkwardly on top of him, I couldn't think of how this night could possibly become any worse or any better at the same time. I snuck a whiff at the base of his collar, and unfortunately the sneak wasn't stealthy enough; Dunstan looked up at me with slight amusement at my half-closed eyes.

"I'm so sorry, Mr. Moab. Really, I am." I sprang up off of him and eyed the traitorous kitten observing us, purring and looking quite comfortable in its surroundings, no longer terrified. As if it understood, it skirted over to me and nuzzled my leg, to say thank you and sorry at the same time, before taking off toward the woods. When I turned back to Dunstan to try to help him up, he was smiling widely, and he broke out into a hearty laugh upon catching sight of the evil eye I threw the kitten as it disappeared into the brush.

My hair had gotten loose, and I was covered in leaves and bits of vine. I dusted myself off as he sprang lightly to his feet, a chuckle still on his lips. My shame was slowly disappearing because I couldn't help but take in some of the humor that he was enjoying at my expense. I had to either cry or laugh at the turn of events, so I chose the latter. As we both righted ourselves and got as much debris off of us as possible, I again became distinctly aware of my proximity to him, and when he reached to take a twig from hair, I almost fainted.

There was a brief moment of awkward silence between us as he stared down at me with inquisitive eyes. "Well, we better head back," he said as he reached to take some more shrubbery from my hair.

It might have been my imagination, but I was sure that his hand lingered a little longer than necessary at the side of my face.

"Any broken parts?" he asked.

"No, I don't believe so," I replied.

"Okay, great. I'll take you to the edge of the woods—I have to finish my run."

"Really, I'm fine; you don't have to," I replied, trying to get away from his gaze without swooning. As the words tumbled out, I felt the warmth rising to my cheeks; it was like his eyes held me in a trance.

"Yeah, but I want to," he replied, his eyes darkening. He inched toward me just enough to make me feel faint. The walk was quiet and quick, and as we emerged from the woods, we heard a light meowing nearby. He threw his head back and laughed again as I cringed and then waved me off in the direction of the building.

Before he left, I remembered the night before. "Oh, Mr. Moab, thank you for dinner," I said coolly.

"No problem. I'm just so sorry that you all had to work that evening and couldn't join us for dinner. It was a pleasant surprise to see you there. I guess you finished early? It's the least that I could do," he finished.

I decided that I wouldn't rat out Vera; not saying anything just seemed like the mature thing to do, so I simply nodded. He kept in the shadows as I turned and jogged back to the building. I suspected that the reason he'd opted to continue with his run was that he was very well aware of the ensuing scandal that would arise if we both emerged from the wooded area, covered in brush, near midnight.

As I rounded the side of the building, I ran straight into Ethan. "What on earth happened to you?" he asked with one eyebrow raised, eyeing my disheveled appearance.

"You wouldn't believe me if I told you." I started to tell him the whole story, but I noticed a glint in his eye that I couldn't quite place. So instead I offered him the simpler explanation about rescuing a cat.

"A cat, you say?" he asked, as if he didn't believe my story. "Well, where is it?" He peering around me and over into the woods.

I cringed at the question because now I would have to explain more than I wanted to. Then, as if on cue, the cat sauntered in and wrapped a lazy tail around my ankle. It meowed softly as I bent to pick it up. I looked back toward the woods, and I was certain that I saw Dunstan in his gray sweatshirt in retreat. I smiled and pushed the little kitten at Ethan. "Here it is."

Ethan recoiled, and I remembered that he was allergic. "Okay," he said. "Well, as cute as he is, I'm not sure how he can stay with us. You know that." He turned and left.

I looked at the adorable creature now staring into my eyes and mimicked Ethan's last words. I knew, though, that he was right. I lifted the kitten higher and returned the stare.

Turns out "it" was a "he," and he pawed my face playfully and then yawned, slightly trembling. "Well, Mr. Kitty, what do we do with you now?" I said more to myself than to the seemingly bored cat. I tucked him under my shirt and headed toward the train, where we were bunking for the night. We were scheduled to depart in less than an hour, and I wondered briefly where Dunstan was now. The scent of him stuck on me, and I wondered whether Ethan had picked it up too or it was all just in my head. I looked at the kitten once more and headed into the building toward the expansive buffet to pick up some milk and a tuna sandwich.

My short trip back to the train was uneventful, and I found myself wishing that somehow I would run into Dunstan again. Back in my cabin on the train, I had no choice but to smile as I watched the kitten practically drown himself in the saucer of milk and then viciously devour the tuna in the sandwich. His little belly was so full when he finished that it looked distended. I attempted to give him a bath, knowing that he would eventually find his way into my bed in the cramped space that we would be sharing for the night. A few minor scratches later, he looked at me through crossed eyes and bathed himself again.

I picked from my hair the last pieces of the night's adventure and took a quick shower. Mr. Kitty, who had cleaned himself from head to toe, then made his way to my pillow and watched me through slightly closed eyes. He yawned again, his eyes getting heavier with each minute. Every now and then, he would shake his head, as if trying to shake the sleepiness away. I laughed out loud when he finally tumbled into an unceremonious heap, with a tiny snore rumbling through his little body. It already felt like he was my pet.

Sitting on the bed, I looked around. My clothes needed to be sorted, and it was then and there that I decided I needed to put down roots somewhere—life had to mean more than this; there had to be more than how I existed currently. I was grateful for everything that I had been blessed with; I just longed for something more, something more settled. I felt as though a piece of me was missing, which caused me never to really fit anywhere. My existence was a series of days rolling into nights that catapulted into mornings. My purpose felt undefined.

I finished the last of my report for the Milan stop and fell into my bed, waking the sleeping cat but only for a minute. He stretched his tiny legs, walked around in a circle, and found a nice warm spot against my cheek, and we both promptly fell asleep.

That night I dreamed of snow and flowers and surfing massive waves.

Chapter 3

———⟨ww⟩⟨o⟩⟨e⟩⟨o⟩⟨o⟩⟨ww⟩———

Dunstan's mind wandered back to his encounter with Destiny. He had stayed back and watched her retreat into the building with the little kitten following closely behind. His heart raced, and he felt exhilarated at meeting her again so soon. As he ran, his mind retreated to the first time they had met. He had gone surfing one day after school just before one of his finals. He was caught in a barrel, executing a perfect 180/360. The winds were offshore, and surfing conditions were ideal. A few spongers were closer to shore, but basically, he was on his own, or so he thought. In a split second, another surfer dropped on him, almost knocking him off the board. He yelled angrily while trying to avoid the unavoidable wipeout he was about to endure. He was locked into the crashing wave when he saw the surfer dive under and swim toward him. The surfer grabbed his leash and hoisted him to the surface, but this just put them both in the impact zone, being pounded.

They both ate ocean, and it was only when they resurfaced a few minutes later that Dunstan realized his anger was targeted at the most beautiful girl he had ever seen. She was sincerely apologetic, and there was little he could say but "okay," so overwhelmed was he by her beauty and her strength to endure such a pounding.

"Are you okay?" he asked, shaking the water from his black hair, which was now slicked to his skull. His eyes burned from the salt water, and his lips were pumped from almost drowning when he and the girl collided.

"Yeah, I'm really sorry, but I didn't see you," she said, a little too loudly. "Looks like you got a pretty nasty gash there." She pointed to his torn suit where purple dots of blood were already leaking through. "I'm really sorry."

"It happens. No worries. Listen, are you sure you're okay? I've got classes in a few, but I don't want to leave if you're hurt," he said, his voice hoarse from the gallon of salt water he'd ingested.

She nodded that she was fine, so he turned and paddled to shore, passing Pete, his fellow classmate on this way. When he got to shore, he turned and saw them on their boards paddling back into the surf. He couldn't shake the vision of her from his mind.

For the rest of the day, he found himself thinking about her occasionally and laughed at himself for being smitten with her so easily. There was a meteor shower that night and his friend Ayala had invited him to a bonfire later that evening, and he felt that the cool ocean breezes were exactly what he needed to free his mind. He got there just when the others were arriving, and after greeting both his friend Pete and Ayala, who were already engaged in close conversation, he found a spot facing the fire, set back from the crowd and its banter and laughter. A group of girls, including an attractive and chatty blonde, plopped beside him, making small talk every now and then. He was polite and responded when necessary, but he found his mind still wandering to the girl he had been thinking about all day. Looking around, he noticed someone leaning back from the crowd, actually looking up at the meteor shower that they were there to watch. Even though she appeared to be there on her own, she seemed comfortable and at ease. It was then that it hit him: someone was silently sharing music with him. The notes were like strokes of a paintbrush in his head. The crescendos of the woodwind, brass, and percussion were tamed with celestas and strings. They wove a pattern of blue and orange with shards of lavender and white light through his head.

"*That's absolutely beautiful,*" he said, looking around to see if anyone there would react to his silent message. The girl watching the meteor shower snapped up suddenly and looked around. He looked straight ahead at her and spoke again without moving his lips.

"*Hi,*" he said softly. "*My name is Dunstan. I'm sorry to intrude, but your music—it's fantastic.*"

"Hi, I'm Destiny," she replied. "*My friends call me Desti.*"

Pete, who was sitting on the opposite side of the fire from Dunstan, shot a look across to them both, and Destiny chuckled.

"*My brother Pete is about to have a heart attack, I believe.*" She smiled. Destiny shifted positions, and the light from the fire caught her face. Dunstan couldn't believe his eyes—it was his mystery surfer, the one he had thought about all day, and she was his classmate's sister too, apparently. He could hardly contain himself.

Pete smiled slightly and winked at Dunstan. "*You and me—we need to talk, later.*" With that, he turned his full attention back to Ayala.

"*I'm sorry that I butt in,*" Dunstan said, "*but the music, it was … well … it is fantastic, and I had to say something. It was more of a thought out loud; I didn't know whether anyone would hear me.*"

She smiled. "*Thanks. You're new to school, right?*"

"*Yeah, joined last semester. I've been trying to get up to speed with everything,*" Dunstan replied.

"*I am too.*" She paused. "*So how does this work for you?*" she asked. "*Can you hear everything?*"

"*Well, only what you want me to hear. It's rare for me to hear without being invited. I'm not sure what happened before when you were thinking about your music—I just heard it and then thought out loud, and you heard me. I wasn't really expecting that.*"

"*Yeah, I tend to leave my doors wide open when I compose. I pick up other teles sometimes,*" she replied.

"*Doors?*" Dunstan asked.

"*Yeah, it's the best way that I can describe how I let people 'hear' me when I want them to,*" Destiny replied.

Just then the chatty blonde leaned over to whisper something into Dunstan's ear. Destiny smiled and refocused her attention on the stars above.

Without warning, Dunstan got up, seemingly oblivious to the girls who were vying for his attention. He walked to the other side of the bonfire, plopping down beside Destiny to the dismay of a chatty blonde and her friends.

"I figure it would be best for us to actually have a conversation before people think that we are both weird," he said aloud, his smile wide.

She stared at him for a moment and then averted her eyes, embarrassed, when she apparently realized she was doing it. "Yes," she agreed. "Hey, I'm sorry about this morning—you know, the almost drowning thing," she said shyly.

"Forgotten," he responded with a grin.

"It's just that I haven't seen the ocean for so long, I left my common sense somewhere between the jeep and the first wave."

"It's cool," he replied, continuing to stare at her. She looked back at him curiously, as if wondering what he was thinking.

Dunstan caught Pete glancing at them every now and then, but on the whole, he seemed totally focused on Ayala.

"My name is Dunstan," he said once again, extending his hand in a most chivalric manner.

She took his hand and smiled shyly. "I'm Destiny, but like I said, my friends call me Desti for short."

"So … how old are you, Desti, you said that you were at Cal Ed U too?" Dunstan asked, directing a nervous glance at her brother.

"Ignore him," she said. "I'll be eighteen next December." She smiled shyly as he drew closer to her. "I was invited to join last semester to major in music composition. Pete is in his full-on big-brother mode; you gotta love him."

Dunstan smiled, saluted Pete, and gave him a thumbs-up. Pete's scowl did not dissipate, and Destiny laughed.

"What are you studying?" she asked.

"Advanced physics. Pete and I share a few classes together. I joined a few weeks ago." They paused as another blast of the shower filled the evening sky. Dunstan tried to concentrate on the sky above but found himself tracing the smooth lines of Destiny's neck as she looked up into the sky. She looked like she had been painted by a master artist. Her hair blew in the breeze, and every now and then, she would tuck a loose tendril behind her ear. She seemed oblivious to the effect that she was having on him, and he enjoyed that.

"So besides producing masterpieces, what else do you like to do?" he asked eventually.

"Well, some think I'm a pretty good surfer …"

When he rolled his eyes, she kicked sand at him, and they both laughed. She went on to tell him about the apartment that she and Pete shared and revealed that she was already fluent in Italian and Japanese. To his delight, she even shared a few sentences in Italian and Japanese. They talked about the school, their gifts, and things they liked and disliked. After some cajoling, he told her that he wrote poetry in his spare time, and outside of surfing, he also enjoyed hiking, but travel was his real hobby.

"I've lived in Europe for most of my life, and I think I inherited my love of physics from my dad. I was invited to join the school two years earlier but I took some time off, traveled a bit," he said. Their conversation was honest and wide-ranging, and they learned more about each other in the few hours than most learned in months of dating.

They took some time out to catch a few more glimpses of the meteor shower shooting across the sky, and as the night went on, they found themselves sitting closer, totally engrossed in each other, oblivious to the glances directed at them. She shivered lightly as the hour grew late, and Dunstan offered her his coat. She sniffed it openly in front of him and rolled her eyes, feigning a swoon as she teased him about the girls in his and her brother's fan club. He laughed when he looked across the fire.

It was just after 12:00 a.m. when Pete approached to tell her that it was time to go because they both had early classes. She stood up to fold her blanket, and Dunstan reached down to help her. His hand covered hers as he helped fold the blanket, and he let it linger for slightly longer than necessary.

"I'd like it very much if I could see you again sometime soon," he said, still holding her hand. "I mean, that is, if you want to. I would love to hear more of your music."

"I'd like that too."

He bent his head and kissed her gently on the cheek and then turned to leave, just barely catching the scowl on her brother's face. A few yards away, Dunstan looked back and saw Destiny watching him leave, her palm held to the spot where he'd kissed her. Dunstan barely took notice of the leggy blonde and her friends standing behind Destiny with their jaws in their sand.

"Come on, lovebird," Ayala chirped, joining Dunstan. "Let's get you home before you swoon." Pete's protective scowl reappeared once again and remained even when Ayala flashed him a brilliant smile. Ayala laughed out loud as she shuffled Dunstan to the path.

Dunstan slowed down as the memories of Destiny's and his early romance flooded his mind. After a minute, he became aware of another presence and turned warily to face his friend Pete on the same path. They continued running together.

"Dunstan, what are you doing? This isn't part of the plan," Pete said, stopping Dunstan with a gentle hand on the shoulder, which drooped at the touch and slight reprimand.

Dunstan inhaled deeply and exhaled slowly before answering. "I know, but I just can't wait anymore. She is right here, and each day that goes by feels like a million years. I didn't plan to meet her here tonight on this running trail. I was going after Charm."

"Who you let wander off with her!" Pete replied.

"I'll get him back; you know I will," Dunstan replied.

"What really is your plan, Dunstan?"

Dunstan resumed running without offering an answer, simply because he had none.

"Dunstan?" Pete asked again. "Look, I know that you want to be with her—we all do—but look at the toll it's taking on your body. Until we get this all figured out, you are playing not only with her life but with yours as well.

"What is your plan—you meet up, maybe you ask her out, maybe you two fall in love again in this dimension, and then what? You can't stay here, and we don't know if we can get her over there. What is your plan, Dunstan?" Pete was now becoming more agitated. "Dunstan, I'm talking to you!"

"And I hear you, Pete." Dunstan stopped his run and turned to face him. "I don't have the answers for you, but I do know this: we've been searching for Destiny for seven years. Seven years of all of our lives we have dedicated to bringing her home, and I am never giving up. Do you hear me? Never."

Dunstan turned and slumped on a nearby bench, suddenly feeling more tired than he had in a long time. He put his head in his hands, as Pete came to sit next to him. Pete filled their minds with thoughts of their childhood, when they were all together. He took them back to the days of surfing huge waves and the nights under the stars.

"*Get out of my head, bro,*" Dunstan said without moving his lips, though he had to admit that the memories had lifted his spirits somewhat.

"*You know that I love my sister,*" Pete said silently. "*She is the only relative that I have left outside of Ayala. No one wants her back more than I do. But I will never forget the pain that she went through when we lost our parents. She couldn't handle it. In fact, that's why she is here today; indeed, it's the reason we all are where we are in our lives.*"

"*Pete, I know this. I was there, front and center, but what am I supposed to do? What if something happens to her here, or to us before she knows? What if we aren't here to help her through this?*"

"*That's my point, Dunstan. What if something does happen to us? To you? You know that you've been aging faster than the rest of us each time you jump—because you have been taking too many risks, jumping too soon and staying too long outside of the parameters we set. We've found her now; we have people watching her practically day and night. You don't need to be here as much now; you don't need to take these chances.*"

"*Wait a minute. Did my dad put you up to this little powwow?*" Dunstan asked suddenly, rising to face Pete.

"*If he did, he would be right. We are all worried about losing you, Dunstan. Think about Destiny—what it might do to her if she gets close to you and then you disappear from her life? All I'm asking you to do is wait just a little while longer before doing anything rash. The tests are almost complete; we may have a solution yet.*"

Dunstan sighed. He knew that Pete was right. "Okay," he finally said out loud. "And keep out of my head. Us sitting here talking like this—it's freaking out the animals." And with that he and Pete continued on the trail. After a while, when they were both out of sight, Ethan emerged from the shadows and headed back to the building.

Chapter 4

T he next morning, I noticed a small envelope had been slipped under my door. I opened it absently, assuming it was work-related. However, to my surprise, inside was a penned invitation from Dunstan, asking me to join him in his cabin later that evening for dinner. My heart did a flip-flop over itself, and I called Ethan immediately. He arrived in my doorway in a few minutes.

"What do you think that this is all about?" I asked.

Ethan was silent for a moment. "Well, I don't know, Desti. I guess that you will have to go and find out." He had a faraway look in his eyes as he continued. "Look, Desti, you and I have been friends for a while now, and I think that we can be honest with each other. You know that I only have the best intentions for you. To put it as simply as I can, Dunstan and you, you're from different worlds." He paused and watched me carefully. He sat on my bed, eyeing Mr. Kitty, ensuring that he kept as far away as possible,

"Wow, where on earth is this coming from? It's a dinner meeting." I laughed at his pensive mood. "Lighten up." In reality though, my heart hadn't stopped pounding since the moment I saw Dunstan's invitation. "Just because he is Dunstan Moab doesn't make him an alien from another world," I said, scooting Mr. Kitty off the bed and sitting beside Ethan.

Ethan smiled faintly. "That's not what I'm saying, Desti." The train's whistle sounded, and there was a slight lurch as the train pulled out from the station. "I'm saying that your life is here, now, with us. I don't want to see you hurt, that's all."

The kitten peeked out of the bathroom where he had retreated and quietly jumped into my lap.

Ethan stood when he saw the feline again. "I know that you aren't serious with keeping this thing here, Desti." Ethan shook his head and rose to leave.

"I know, I know … I just haven't figured out what to do with him as yet. I'll take care of him at the next stop," I said, scooping him up. I already loved him and couldn't bear the thought of parting with him so soon. Ethan left shortly after and the rest of the day passed uneventfully, with Mr. Kitty doing everything that he could, it seemed, to wrestle smiles from me.

At 7:25 p.m., I stood a bit nervously at Dunstan's door. Since I was joining him in his cabin, I figured it would be a pretty casual dinner, mirroring the mode of delivery of the invitation. I had chosen a white cotton shirt to top my favorite jeans. I tapped lightly on the door, and when Dunstan opened it, he paused and gave me an appreciative smile before ushering me in. I was glad that I had followed my instinct because he too was casual in a pair of faded Dockers and a light blue shirt, which seemed to make his gray eyes appear bright blue. His cabin took up two cars with a lounge and dining area in one and a bedroom in the other. The smooth sounds of an Anita O'Day's remake cooed from a sound system near the television, which itself was on mute but showing a football match. The cabin was warm, cozy, relaxed, and comforting.

Soon, we were chattering away as Dunstan showed me the collection of music that he had brought with him. He told me that this was but a small piece of his collection; he was an avid music fan. We almost didn't hear the light tap on the door, which

Dunstan rose to answer after possibly the third or fourth tap. Standing in the doorway, Vera looked surprised by my presence but said nothing. Her skirt was a little too tight, and she was wearing way too much makeup for the occasion, yet she waltzed in with her smile and charm on full blast.

"Vera, it's good to see you. Thank you for joining me at such short notice," Dunstan said. "Dinner is ready, so we might as well dig in." Vera moved to his side, but he casually placed his hand on the small of my back and guided me to a chair beside his. Once I was seated, he held a chair for Vera on the opposite side of the table.

Vera acted as though the subtle snub hadn't happened and said brightly, "Right, I'm starving."

I had never seen this side of Dunstan before. He chatted all through dinner and seemed rejuvenated and well rested. Occasionally, he would brush my arm, and I had to admit that I was enjoying the company thoroughly, despite Vera's sullen, quiet mood. When she did speak, she directed her conversation to Dunstan, intentionally ignoring my presence, but that didn't bother me one bit because I felt at ease with Dunstan and the effort he was making to involve me. Eventually her contributions to the conversation waned so much that she practically said nothing at all, and I was wondered if she was pouting and picking at her food because her skirt was just too tight.

As our plates were being cleared, Dunstan turned down the volume of the music and began speaking in a more serious tone. "So, Vera and Destiny, the reason I have invited you both here tonight is that I am going to implement a few changes to ease the workload not only of your respective teams but also, I think, of the company on the whole. We also want to take advantage of new and burgeoning talent that's permeating the company. I'm putting a hold on the expansion program." He paused and turned his attention to me for a moment. "I think that I've found what I'm looking for to move forward with the company. I want us to spend some time investing in what we have now.

"We have more than enough offices to hold our own. We are a unique company, and you both have done exceptionally well in your respective areas of expertise. Of course, this means some changes for your teams, so I wanted to share my plan with you." His eyes became dark and serious, and the corporate Dunstan that I was familiar with resurfaced.

"An opportunity will soon arise for a new leadership post in the European office. Destiny, I want you to apply. I've been tracking your performance over the last year or so, and I see great potential in you. This is why I think that you should consider the position in Italy. It's a big jump from what you are doing now, but I have every confidence in your ability."

I had picked up my glass of water and was mid-gulp when he said this, and I felt the sticking pain of water and air going down the wrong way at the same time, but I was able to control it. "You want me to head the European operations team?" I asked incredulously.

"Yes," he calmly replied.

Vera's face lit up. "Desti, I know that this is something you can do. You are a trooper; I'm sure that you can handle being over here on your own." Her mood had lifted dramatically. She would be glad to have me far away from her (and Dunstan) and whatever plans she had already started to cook in her head.

"Well, she won't be alone," Dunstan said, staring directly into my eyes as he spoke. "She'll be with me. I'll mentor her myself." Vera's dessert fork clanged against her plate, but she plastered a smile on her face as Dunstan continued to lay out his plan for us both.

Once he was done, the rest of the dinner was spent in relative silence. I thanked Dunstan for the opportunity, but Vera's scowl overshadowed my gratitude. I rose to leave with her at the end of the meal, but Dunstan asked if I would remain with him to discuss the changes he'd proposed. He escorted a disappointed Vera out the door, and she said nothing to me as she left. After he closed the door behind her, Dunstan and I sat on the couch and sipped on mugs of coffee.

"Do you think that she will get over herself?" Dunstan asked with a playful smirk.

"Oh, I don't know. I think that you broke her heart," I replied, nervously fumbling with the button on my shirt, still giddy from the night's events.

Dunstan threw his head back and laughed heartily. "I'm sure that she will get over it. The question is, are you okay with all of this?"

"Of course I am. I mean, it would be a wonderful opportunity, and I'm so grateful. But I am not sure why you chose me," I said.

"I believe that you will bring a fresh perspective to getting things done. You are versed in many cultures that I am sure you will work out well. This is what Dream Scape Inc. is all about—finding talent, cultivating it, and then utilizing its full potential. Besides, it's you that I want—not anyone else."

"I don't know what to say," I said softly, not really sure whether his last statement was lined with an innuendo or whether it was just my imagination.

"Say you'll at least go through the recruitment process - do the research – we'll make it transparent and fair to any other candidate," he said, grasping my hand.

"Let me think about it for a bit," I said. I contemplated it for all of three seconds before saying okay—which Dunstan seemed to find extraordinarily funny. For the next hour or so, Dunstan and I hammered out the logistics of his plan, in between light laughter. Surprisingly, we touched on some personal topics too. I told him of Mr. Kitty's temporary home in my cabin and his antics in the discovery of the litter box I had created for him on the morning after my bungled rescue attempt.

"He pounces on it and then waits until I either turn around or leave before he uses it. It's the funniest thing to watch. I know that I can't keep him, and I'll be heartbroken to part with the little mongrel," I said.

We spent the next hour or so going through some more details, and it seemed as though Dunstan was feeling me out to see how I would organize my team if I were successful in acquiring the position. It must have been well after eleven when I had to stifle my second yawn for the evening. Dunstan offered to call it a night, studying me with brooding, beautiful eyes.

It was Dunstan's idea to walk me back to my cabin. Although dinner was no longer being served, many of the team members were still in the dining car, much to my dismay, and we had no choice but to walk past at least twenty pairs of inquisitive eyes. It didn't help either that he was especially breathtaking in his casual getup—he seemed more reachable, like he wasn't out there among the stars anymore. I could feel Vera's icy gaze following us through the cabin as she openly glared at us from the same table with Ethan and Stella. The couple seemed only absently interested in us as we passed through, but I did notice that Stella had a look in her eye that I couldn't quite interpret.

"Destiny, there is nothing to hide. Don't worry about what Vera thinks or what anyone else thinks for that matter," he whispered as if he could read my thoughts.

"Okay."

Dunstan smiled as I stiffened my back and walked through the dining car at his side. It was hushed in the usual way that it was when Dunstan walked into any room, but to me the silence was deafening. At my cabin door, Dunstan slid the door open for me and looked at me intently, his dreamy eyes pulling me into a vortex. "You'll be just fine."

He bade me good night with a light kiss on my cheek. I slipped inside and tried to keep the final moment of our good-bye etched in my brain. Given the way that he looked at me sometimes, I wondered whether his feelings for me were growing as exponentially as mine were. I convinced myself that he was only trying to help me out.

Over the following days, I spent most of my time in my cabin researching the new post, its people, and what would be expected of me. Dunstan was caught up in his stops, and on the one or two occasions that I was able to catch a glimpse of him, he smiled politely.

The kitten spent his days and nights in my cabin, and although he never complained for sustenance—he enjoyed the constant supply of yummy food and snacks—I felt guilty for keeping him locked up all the time, so at every stop I would let him outside with me as I emptied his litter. Luckily, we stopped two or three times a day; otherwise, the stench would have been overpowering, considering our close living quarters.

On most nights I dined alone in my cabin. It wasn't that I didn't want the company of Ethan and the others, but more so that I suddenly only wanted to be in the company of Dunstan. Each day I found myself daydreaming of him, wishing that he were near me, that we could share a moment, a laugh, or a memory.

Unfortunately, however, when he wasn't doing the conferences, he would disappear into meetings. I knew how tight his schedule was, so I bided my time until the next possible rendezvous—at least that's how I was thinking of our meetings.

A few days ahead of the scheduled end of this leg of the tour, Ethan and I had dinner together. The energy between us felt strained, and though I didn't understand why, he volunteered no more information than he had already. He seemed extra-caring and extra-cautious, and he gave off an air of foreboding as he reiterated subtle comments on Dunstan and the 'lifestyles of the rich and famous'. For the first time since we'd become friends, I was anxious to be through with our dinner. I had received an e-mail from Dunstan asking me to join him for drinks in his cabin with a few of the directors of the European office. We had exchanged some light banter about him using me for my language skills since half the time he couldn't understand anything that the directors were saying. Ethan seemed to sense my impatience and waved me off like a kid on a first date before finishing his meal. I hurriedly returned to my cabin, fed Mr. Kitty, and decided to change into something a bit more formal for the evening.

I chose a fitted dress that rose just above my knee and a pair of nude stilettos—nothing too sexy, yet I wasn't too drab-looking either. Mr. Kitty looked at me with bored eyes as he licked himself from head to toe, but he paused long enough to give me what seemed like an appreciative nod. I floated through the door.

As I arrived at Dunstan's cabin, I could hear the chatter on the other side of the door. I was greeted with a huge smile as Dunstan ushered me in, and I was caught up in the conversation almost immediately. It was a fun and relaxing evening as three other contenders for the position in Italy and I took notes on the expectations of the post. I noticed that Vera stayed as close as possible to Dunstan throughout the evening and said little or nothing to me. It bothered me for a bit, but I was glad to be in the presence of Dunstan and the people I might be working with in the very near future. At the end of the evening, I was sure that I had impressed everyone there enough to be the top pick, and I left feeling both exhilarated but disappointed that I hadn't been able to spend any real quality time with Dunstan.

Chapter 5

———∿∿⋐⊙⋑⋐⊙⋑⊙∿∿———

The next day, I realized that I'd left my notebook in Dunstan's cabin. It was early in the morning—barely after six—so I thought that I would grab a quick bite before venturing back to Dunstan's cabin to retrieve it. Although I was unsure why, I decided to walk past Dunstan's cabin first and then head back to the dining cabin. Just as I was about to turn around, I heard the door slide open, and I cringed at the sound of Vera's voice. I turned slightly and saw her pause just outside of Dunstan's door and lean back in for a few seconds, probably to exchange a farewell kiss. As she passed me, I noticed that she was wearing the same clothes as the night before. She smiled as she walked past, with a lightness to her step.

"Oh, hi, Destiny, you're up early," she said absently, as if seeing me for the first time. "Dunstan asked me to give this to you. Guess you forgot it last night." She handed me my notebook. "It's cute," she added, referring to the doodles I had scribbled across it.

I thanked her for it and turned and headed in the other direction, hearing her squeaky but expensive heels echoing against the carpeting. I was no longer confused, and I decided to bow out of a race that I wasn't even sure that I was a part of.

It was 5:00 a.m. two days later when I heard the panicked and hushed voices outside my cabin, and my curiosity was piqued enough that I opened the small window to see what was going on. I grabbed a coat and disembarked. The rest of the team was standing outside, still in their pajamas and coats but fully immersed in their communication devices. I checked my phone and noticed a series of messages referencing "Dunstan's Route Change."

"It's just him," Ethan said. "No one seems to know what's up. This is our last stop, and we return to the US tomorrow. Dunstan has to take an unexpected trip and is canceling the tour with still five more stops to go." Ethan tumbled over his words as if he couldn't catch his breath. "All hell breaks loose for us in a few hours."

We would have our work cut out for us. I was a bit miffed. The good thing about it, however, was that for the morning at least, I would have a few hours free, and that gave me time to figure out what to do about Mr. Kitty, who was still sleeping peacefully despite the commotion.

An hour or so later, as I returned to the train with Mr. Kitty after our usual outdoor romp, a sheet of paper being pushed around by the breeze brushed my leg. I bent down and picked it up; it was a flyer for a local animal rescue shelter. I looked at Mr. Kitty with a heavy heart. I took him to the shelter as soon as it opened since the train was scheduled to depart in the evening, with one more stop before we headed back to the airport. I had decided that now was as good a time as any, and the girl behind the desk of the neat, efficient-looking office seemed nice enough as she looked Mr. Kitty over. She had an Australian twang that made me giggle. Mr. Kitty practically bounded out of my arms to her, and that consoled me; I felt that she would find a good home for him. I left as large a donation as I could and asked that he be given the best possible care. She was kind enough to take my e-mail address so that she could send me a picture of Mr. Kitty in his new home when the time came.

As we parted, he looked directly at me with his intelligent blue eyes. I hugged him gently and wistfully one time, wishing that I had a more stable environment so that I could keep him, and he pawed me lightly on the cheek the way he had when we first met. He meowed quietly once, nuzzled me, and then turned his attention to the catnip lying on the floor next to the office scratching post. I sighed and left. I was already attached, and I ached to keep him, but I knew that I couldn't.

I returned to the train feeling alone. I wasn't sure which had bummed me out more, losing Mr. Kitty or the smug look on Vera's face as she left Dunstan's cabin a few days before. Either way, I was pretty depressed.

Within a few days of our return to the United States, I learned that I had been short-listed for the position that Dunstan had spoken to me about on the train. I hadn't seen Dunstan Moab since the last meeting in his cabin, and my initial fascination from our first meeting had waned a bit. But every now and then over the next week, when there was a sudden buzz in the office, my heart did a tiny flip-flop as I secretly hoped that Dunstan would walk through the door. This never happened. But by the end of the week, I received confirmation that I'd been awarded the new position.

I said my farewells at a small seaside bar in Northern California. My team filled the bar with camaraderie and laughter, and every now and then, someone pulled out a funny story about me. I was sad to be parting from the people that I had worked with over the years, but at the same time, I looked forward to a new and more settled life in Italy. Vera even called—during "a dinner engagement," she said—to bid me farewell, and I closed the book on whatever hope I'd held out for me and Dunstan upon finding out that she was out with him again that night.

My good-byes complete, I hightailed it back to Italy, determined to be successful and progress even further in the company. I was collected from the airport by one of the company drivers, and I was awed by the beauty of the countryside as we drove toward the Tuscany offices. When we arrived at our destination, my jaw dropped; the corporate offices of Dream Scape Inc. in Italy resembled a resort more than a place of business. The photos I had seen online did not do the actual location any real justice. As I looked up at the rock facade, it felt like I was in a valley of sorts and the buildings were etched right into the hillside. The main building was stately yet welcoming. It was cast out of rock, and yellow lights peeped out like eyes, as if welcoming visitors. There was a fabulous fountain with purple flowers spilling over its base, and the pathway was made of weathered stone. The wind gently whistled in the trees, and I could hear the faint songs of birds as they made their way home. The entire facility felt old and new at the same time. I found it very comforting.

I made my way inside. In my years with the company, I had seen some fantastic sights, but the elegance and dreamlike atmosphere of this place overtook me. Gigantic posts flanked the entrance. They looked like they had been transported in time from the Roman era, and an intricate design of leaves and vines was etched into each post. The center of the roof was high, at least three to four stories, and made of pure, seamless glass. In splendid grandeur, the walls were constructed of polished granite and marble, which shone as if only recently installed.

The entire floor was tiled with a luxurious marble, tastefully done with subtle hues so that it didn't feel overdone or gaudy. Oversized chaise lounges flanked expansive arched windows. Soft lamps were strategically placed, giving the whole area an ethereal glow. Beside each chair was a circular glass-top table with reading materials, and peeking closer, I saw blankets folded neatly on shelves beneath each glass top. Hanging from the ceiling was a grand chandelier, and I was captivated by the glass and crystals twinkling in the setting sun. The rest of the building felt as though it had been carved into the rock face. There was a majestic water feature in the center, with stone dolphins flanking the shooting water. The water was pristine, and the sound of the water was muted—just enough to calm yet enthrall those who entered the building. Everything here felt so fantastic yet familiar.

I was greeted by one of the administrative clerks, who turned on his Italian charm almost instantly. He gave me a quick tour of the building, which included an office overlooking the Tuscan countryside. Once we were through, he offered to lead me to my new home. We exited the building and headed back to the parking lot, where he pointed out the company car assigned to me and handed me the keys, and then we started out for the short ride uphill. The unique aspect of this Dream Scape location was that it also housed many of its employees. The hills were dotted with residences, and I was delighted to know that I also would be partaking in the beautiful sunrises and brilliant sunsets in the Tuscan hills. I followed the clerk uphill in my newly assigned car, and as my mind cleared from the buzz below, I took in the sights around me. The company's property line seemed unbounded as we climbed higher. I loosened my hair and leaned out the window slightly to let the crisp air fill my lungs. The higher up we climbed, the freer I began to feel. The air was so clean, and I could hear a waterfall in the distance. As the sun dipped in the horizon, a chill began to blanket the landscape.

Soon, we pulled into a small circular driveway. We disembarked and took the short flowered-covered path to the cutest cottage I had ever seen. It wasn't overly large, but looked homey in the setting sun. The clerk took the rest of my luggage inside and quickly showed me around. He left his number on the table before leaving, and I followed him outside and watched him drive back down the hill. I scanned the panoramic view below, exhaling slowly soaking it all in.

Going back inside to explore the place more, I found the cottage well stocked with groceries, which was another pleasant surprise. While checking out each room, I stopped to look at myself in the somewhat small yet modern and efficient bathroom. Faint circles beneath my eyes were a sign that my time would be better spent catching up on some well-needed rest instead of the constant on-the-go lifestyle I had been living for the past few years.

I took my bag into the kitchen and unpacked some of its contents. I reached for the kettle and filled it with water to brew myself a cup of green tea, which I bought only from my favorite tea shop, Shigetsuen in Japan. I had met the third-generation tea sommelier in the UK the year before and had bought only his brews since then. I kicked my shoes off and sat outside on the porch for a bit. I was exhausted, and my temples were beginning to throb. The tea was the only thing that seemed to help ease the pounding in my skull. It felt as though my headaches had been dully present for as long as I could remember, and in a few minutes, as the tea stewed, I headed to the shower.

After showering, I wrapped myself in a warm blanket from the cottage and stepped outside. I stood in the gardens of my new residence and eyed my surroundings. An oversized chair on the little porch looked out to the valley below, and it was too inviting to ignore. My hair tumbled over my shoulders as I sank into the plush cushion. The breeze blowing across the valley and up the hill had a bit of a nip to it, but it was just too pretty to go inside. I sank deeper into the chair and was asleep in a few minutes. For the first time in as long as I could remember, I felt as though I was at home. I felt safe and happy, and I snuggled deeper into the warm blanket that I had found.

The next day, I decided to explore with an early morning run. I followed the path back down to the main building and ran across the parking lot. It was still pretty early, but already a few people were milling in the front of the building. I waved good morning and ran around the side of the building and to the back. It opened to well-manicured gardens, and casual benches dotted the alcoves created by trellises and arbors. Calmness began to creep into me, and I felt the hectic year of scheduling, planning, traveling, and managing deadlines already beginning to recede. As I rounded a corner to begin my trek back uphill, I saw a handsome man casually slouched on one of the benches, soaking up the early morning sun. He looked vaguely familiar, and I was sure that I had seen him somewhere in the near past, but I couldn't place him. He reminded me of a blond angel, and he seemed to have sensed my presence more than heard me when he opened his eyes and smiled at me. For a split second, I caught a hint of familiarity in the way he looked at me, and then he suddenly looked sad. He nodded and closed his eyes again, seeming to be enthralled by his surroundings.

I finished my run and took a slow walk back to the cottage. I showered and got dressed and was in my car just before 8:00 a.m. to begin my first day. As I waited for the elevator, I turned toward a small commotion behind me. To my surprise, Dunstan Moab had entered the building. Whenever he was around, it was as if royalty had shown up. Everyone spoke in hushed and urgent tones, but I remembered how natural it had felt to talk to him during our encounter in the woods and the first dinner we'd shared back on the train. I had pocketed our meeting in a secret, special place in my mind. Sometimes I caught myself daydreaming of his smile, and I got chills remembering what he felt like beneath me that night in the woods. This vision was cut short, however, when Vera's laughter filled the air.

Then the golden-haired young man I'd seen on my run earlier entered behind Dunstan. Suddenly, my head began to throb. I

had been having unexplained headaches for as long as I could remember, but I was upset that I could feel the onset of one on my first day. The pain didn't stop me, however, from studying the two men in more detail as they talked with one another. They were both beautiful, almost in a celestial sort of way. In a different time and place, one could have been a prince and the other a superhero. They both held the kind of appeal that made people look at them even if they didn't want to, and I chuckled to myself as I imagined them releasing blue light into the air as part of their superhuman-like features. I shook my head and laughed inwardly once again when I realized that every person in the room was either openly staring or sneaking glances at them both, and I was among the gawkers. But the two men seemed oblivious to the effect that they were causing as they continued their conversation in earnest, walking toward me. I turned as the elevator doors pinged open.

Dunstan and his companion entered the elevator with me, and Dunstan stopped his conversation and smiled brightly. "Welcome, Destiny," he said. "I hope that everything is okay here for you."

"Oh, yes indeed. Thank you, Mr. Moab," I replied.

He furrowed his brow at my cool response. "Back on the surnames, are we?" He chuckled as we rode up to the fourth floor and seemed oblivious to how miffed I was that he'd apparently played me while having an affair with my boss. I shook it off and, when the doors opened, headed to my office.

The rest of the day was uneventful, and despite my pounding head, I settled in nicely. There was a measured amount of respect for me in the office since I was the youngest person to have ever been considered for such a position. It didn't hurt that my Italian was fluent and natural—an asset I had over the other international applicants. Shortly after 5:00 p.m., I headed back uphill to my cottage and spent the early evening in comfortable solitude with the setting sun.

There was a welcome event scheduled for me in a few hours, and after fixing myself a quick dinner, I had about an hour to get dressed and head back down. I decided on a Manifattura Donna dress that was professional with just enough sexy to capture attention. I spent a little more time on my makeup than usual, still hoping that I would have another chance encounter with Dunstan. I gave myself a once-over and, liking what I saw, headed back down to the office for the party.

As I entered the grounds, I was greeted by several of my new colleagues, who all commented on my attire and the way I seemed to be glowing. I had no clue what they were talking about, but I soon lost my status as the center of attention, when Dunstan arrived. He came straight to me, his eyes never leaving mine, and I felt warm and out of breath by the time he finished crossing the gardens and stood by my side.

"Hello, Destiny. You look great tonight," he said.

"Thank you, Mr. Moab. It's good of you to come," I replied.

"I wouldn't miss it. You are going to have a huge impact on the people here. I can feel it," Dunstan said, signaling a waiter to bring us some drinks. Dunstan was wearing a pale green shirt that fit him well. It occurred to me that I had never seen him in anything that didn't fit or suit him perfectly. I took a glass of champagne and nodded politely at the waiter.

"Everyone gather around," Dunstan said, raising his glass in toast. "I would like to raise a toast to Miss Destiny Tallum, one of the most talented people here at Dream Scape. I know that she will work wonders here in Europe, and I urge you to give her all of your support. She is here to change lives, not only on this team but for all of us here at Dream Scape." He looked down at me and took a sip, and the rest of the guests followed suit. I wasn't sure whether there was any innuendo in his last statement, but I was already overwhelmed by the show of support that I had received thus far.

For the rest of the evening, Dunstan stayed close to me, introducing me to several people but keeping our conversation light and professional. I too kept my distance, and at times when we were alone and he attempted to lighten the mood, I was sure that I came off as a bit aloof. I had decided, however, that I would not let my schoolgirl crush develop into anything more in my brain. Instead, I would focus on putting my best foot forward. This was a tough enough assignment as it was without me having to worry about gray eyes, pink lips, or sweet, perfect smiles.

"Destiny ... Destiny, are you here with us?" Dunstan asked.

I smiled sweetly as I broke away from my daydream and shifted my attention to the two or three persons who had joined us. I spoke fluently in Italian to them, and they all laughed, thrilled at my fluency, and told me that they were indeed looking forward to working with me. Dunstan remained quiet throughout the conversation, and I could feel his eyes on me as I left his side and moved about among the crowd. By the end of the evening, I had made a mental note of the names of all the people I would be interacting with on a daily basis. Shortly before eleven, as I bade the remaining guests farewell, Dunstan was nowhere to be seen, and although I tried to convince myself that his absence suited me just fine, inside I was sorry that I hadn't gotten a chance to tell him good-bye.

My eyes opened at five the next morning from sheer programming. It was the first time in as long as I could remember that I'd awoken feeling reenergized and rested. It was still dark out, so I snuggled back into bed and daydreamed. Since seeing Dunstan again the day before, I hadn't been able to get him out of my mind; he seemed to intrude on every personal and private thought. The smile that had greeted me in the lobby was imprinted in my brain. I was still pleasantly shocked that he was already here. After a few minutes, I sighed and reached for my e-reader. I needed to get over this, whatever this was, so I delved into the latest novel that I'd started weeks ago but hadn't had the time to complete.

Unfortunately, my mind continued wandering back to Dunstan, and when I realized that I had read the same line about fifty times, I decided that I needed to get up and about. I felt that a quick run would help to clear my head, so I stuck my head outside to gauge the temperature and decided it was pleasant enough. Just outside my door, a sweet aroma invaded my nostrils. My stomach rumbled in complaint, but I left anyway, determining that my run would be over soon, and I would splurge on a big breakfast when I returned. Grabbing an apple, I headed out. I opted to run through the wooded area surrounding my home and was pleasantly surprised to find a trail between the brush and shrubbery. The morning was just beginning to warm, but it was still pleasant enough for me to enjoy my spectacular surroundings. The sun was creeping up through the eastern hills, and occasionally I had to shade my eyes from the glare of the sunrise.

It was so beautiful here. I wanted to see everything at the same time. The smell of the clean air, the woodsy terrain, and the wildflowers thrilled me completely. At one point I turned around and jogged backward, just so I could glimpse the peaceful valley below. I could see the mist from one of the natural waterfalls creating a rainbow and wished I had my phone so that I could capture the scene. As I was about to turn around again, I thudded into something and fell forward onto my belly, scraping my arm and elbow as I tried to break my fall. I had run backward into a tree, I thought. I was trying to right myself when a pair of arms wrapped gently around my waist to help me. I recoiled in horror upon realizing someone had witnessed my graceful collision with a tree and turned to face the person.

It was Dunstan Moab. And from the looks of his sweats, now covered in brush and soil, he was my tree. Again.

Chapter 6

A s he rose and brushed himself off, Dunstan had an
opportunity to digest her beauty. It blew him away each
time he saw her. After all this time, little had changed
about her. Her eyes shone and reflected everything she looked at.
Her skin was the color of milk chocolate, and the dark brown hair
framing her face enhanced the pink of her pouty lips. Hearing
her voice was like listening to his favorite musician on repeat. Her
beauty was breathtaking, and the fact that she seemed so unaware
of her effect on all around her made her even more irresistible. It
took all of his restraint to not reach out and touch her face to make
sure that he had indeed found her again.

"Oh my goodness, Mr. Moab. I'm so sorry. I didn't see you!"
The words tumbled out as she tried to stand as gracefully as she
could; he saw her wince in pain from what he surmised was a bad
sprain. "We seem to keep bumping into each other in the strangest
of places," Destiny said as she brushed herself off.

Watching her shift her weight from one foot to the next, he
could tell that she was in pain as she winced and bit her lip. When
she seemed to have gathered a measure of composure, she looked
him in the eyes, and it was all he could do not to gather her in his
arms to feel the familiarity of her closeness, which he ached for
after all these years.

Instead, he caught her by the arm as she wavered. "I'm fine, but we really should stop meeting this way," he agreed.

"I think that I might have done some damage to my ankle," she said, pursing her lips in evident pain as she touched her shin lightly. He wondered if her injury might be a little worse than she was letting on.

His smile instantly faded, and he asked with concern, "Are you sure you're okay? You also look like you have a bit of a bruise there." He pointed to her hand, which was turning a deeper brown than the rest of her. "I also think that you might have twisted your ankle. Here, do you mind if I help?"

He extended his arm, and she had no choice but to take his hand. "Is this okay?" he asked as he positioned himself so that she could lean into him. They hobbled up the short path in silence, soon arriving at her cottage door.

As they entered the small, cozy living area, Dunstan unstrapped his iPod from the back of his neck and removed his earbuds. He set them on a table and gently moved her to the chair beside the fireplace.

"Do you think you can get the shoe off?" he asked.

She nodded and tried but found that she couldn't without inflicting some serious pain on herself.

"Here, let me help you." In a flash, he was down on his knees, undoing the laces of her sneakers, before she could reposition herself better to continue trying. As he worked to slowly and gently tug the shoe off, she took in a firsthand, close-up view of him.

His face stayed so still as he examined her ankle, and even though he scrunched his eyebrows, his forehead somehow remained seamless. She fought the urge to touch the side of his face or to run her fingers through his hair to see if he was real. The hair that framed his face was jet-black and thick. Talk about a shampoo ad! The fringes on the side of his face were slightly frayed, giving him an almost elf-like look, but the upsweep from his forehead gave him enough edge to scream "model." She winced again as he gently removed her sock, revealing an ankle more injured than she had originally thought. He looked dismayed at the sight of it.

He looked up at her and said, "I'm really sorry, Destiny, but it looks pretty rough; I should get someone to look at it for you."

"I'm sure it's just twisted," she said, suddenly embarrassed at her condition. "I'll ice it, and it'll be back to good in no time." She tried to stand but shrank back into the chair as a wave of pain traveled through her leg. She looked meekly at her toes as she listened to Dunstan on the phone requesting that a doctor be sent to see her. In what seemed to be a short few minutes, a car door slammed, followed by a light tap on the door. The blond man she'd seen twice before stood in the doorway with a look of genuine concern on his face.

"Hi, Pete," Dunstan said. "Here is your patient."

"Let's see what damage you've done, Dunstan," the doctor said with a smile. He turned to her and said kindly and softly, "My name is Pete. I'm just going to take a look at your ankle now, Destiny—is that okay?"

"Yes," she said awkwardly.

The good doctor was also incredibly good-looking, but in a boy-next-door kind of way. He had pale blond hair and stunning blue eyes. His angular features were highlighted by a deep tan. He should be a surfer or an actor, not a doctor. She smiled inwardly as she hoped that she wasn't in some sort of reenactment of a novel, surrounded by beings who were too beautiful to be human and cold to the touch, but the pain shooting through her leg brought her back to reality in a flash.

"Well, Destiny," he said after examining her ankle, "I don't believe it's broken, but it is twisted." He looked over to Dunstan, who was already moving toward the bag Pete had placed on the

51

table. After Dunstan handed him the bag, Pete pulled out a bottle. "Here are a few painkillers," he said. "Take a couple of these now"— he shook two into her hand—"and two more every four hours. You will need to stay off your ankle for the next twenty-four to forty-eight hours. For the next two days, put an ice pack on it for twenty minutes at a time every three to four hours, and make sure that you keep it elevated as much as possible." He took a quick look at the bruise on her hand, cleaned it, and applied a bandage.

Dunstan had stayed back while Destiny was being attended to, but as soon as Pete was finished, he came forward. His eyebrows were furrowed, and he seemed unusually agitated. He gently placed a pack of peas that he had taken from the freezer on her ankle.

"Relax," the doctor said to Dunstan as if answering an unspoken question. "I assure you, her injuries aren't life-threatening." As he stood, a brilliant smile lit up his face.

She closed her eyes, not knowing which mode of death to take—death from embarrassment or death from excitement via her overcharged, pulsating heart. Pete turned and walked with Dunstan to the door. They seemed to be having really low conversations; this was the second time that one seemed to answer the other without Destiny hearing the question. She leaned back into the chair and realized that the painkillers were also affecting the headache that had stayed with her from the day before.

Destiny heard the car door slam and the sound of Pete's vehicle pulling out of the driveway. The sun was now fully up, filling the cottage with warm light.

On his return, Dunstan paused at the doorway, once again in awe of her beauty. The glow of the early morning sun seemed to create a halo effect around her, and even as she sat there disheveled and in pain, his heart raced. She opened her eyes and looked at him through half-closed eyelids. *So sexy*, he thought. They began speaking at the same time, but he stopped to allow her to proceed.

"I'm really sorry for all the trouble; I didn't see you on the path." She could feel the electricity in the room between them, and she couldn't help but openly return his gaze. "To be honest, everything is so beautiful here, and I wanted to take it all in."

He caught her slight innuendo but said nothing as she continued. "I have a habit of running backward. I do that a lot when I'm somewhere new—I try to take everything in as much as I can, and somehow, running backward works for me."

She had no choice but to laugh out loud with him when a chuckle escaped from his lips. He moved closer to prop up the pillow that was now beginning to sag behind her. "Don't beat yourself up about it." He paused only a few inches from her face. "I was doing the same thing," he said with a twinkle in his eye.

They both laughed, and she realized that they were both at ease with each other. The room felt charged with energy, and Destiny still had the indescribable urge to touch his face. Every time he looked at her, she felt mesmerized and she had to remind herself to breathe once again as he casually offered to fix her breakfast.

To her surprise, he whipped up two incredibly-smelling omelets in no time at all, all the while chatting about life in Italy and some of the sights she should try to take in now that she was here. He brought a tray to her and leaned in to once again prop her up. She couldn't help but take a whiff of his hair. She closed her eyes in reverie for just a split second, but she was sure that she was caught in the act. If he noticed, however, he said nothing; he simply smiled.

He sat on the floor directly in front of her, and they continued chatting away as if they were long-lost friends. During their dinner back on the train, Destiny had seen how easy it was for him to shed the CEO persona and just be himself.

She was a great listener, and he already felt as though they had lost nothing in the time apart. He had made her favorite breakfast, and he casually wondered whether anything felt familiar to her. She was still so beautiful and strong, and after all the years he'd spent searching for her, the traits that he loved were still there. As they finished their meal, Dunstan rose from the floor with a crestfallen look on his face; he knew he had to leave. He took her plate and said with true concern in his eyes, "I really do have to get going, but if you need anything, here is my personal cell; call me anytime you like." He scribbled his number on the pad next to the phone and looked at her wistfully once again as she rose to hop with him to the door. As they drew close, she felt more than heard him inhale sharply as he looked down; his eyes grew dark, and suddenly it was as if the background faded as he steadied her. His fingers lingered on her arm a few seconds longer than necessary, leaving a fiery trail in their wake.

"Are you sure that you will be okay?" he asked, releasing her.

"Yes, honestly, I will be okay. Don't worry about me." She tapped her forehead in salute and said, "I'm a soldier—tough as nails."

He smiled. "Well, okay, lieutenant. You take care."

When he smiled at her, she again noticed his stunning, perfectly white teeth. Again she marveled that it was impossible for him to be so gorgeous. Her heart fluttered, and when weakness overtook her entire body, she pretended the cause was the swollen ankle and shifted her weight to the door.

"I'm really sorry, Desti, for causing you pain," he said gently.

She was surprised for a minute at the use of her pet name, which she didn't remember ever telling him; she assumed he must have overheard a member of her former team use it. "It's okay, really," she said as he backed away. "You had better turn around before you crash into something again."

He threw his head back and laughed. "You're absolutely right," he replied. "I hope that this isn't too forward of me, but maybe you would like to join me for a late lunch? I figure that you should be off of that ankle for a few days. I can send for you if you like."

Destiny paused intentionally so as not to show her excitement and confusion at being asked out once again by Dunstan. After a moment, she shrugged it off as him being concerned about her twisted ankle. "Yes, I'd like that."

Chapter 7

———⁓⦿⦿⦿⦿⦿⁓———

After Dunstan left, I reached for my phone, noting that I hadn't checked it yet today. It was well after 9:00 a.m., and several missed calls blinked away. I suddenly realized that I hadn't switched it from silent mode after waking up. Ethan answered his phone on the first ring.

"Desti, are you okay up there? What's going on?" he asked in a hushed whisper. "Where are you? I've been trying to reach you all morning. You've missed two conference calls so far. Are you okay?"

"I'm fine. I'm sorry—I had a bit of an accident." I explained about my twisted ankle.

"I know. I heard," he said rather abruptly. His voice trailed off, and I could hear Vera's in the background, indicating that he had probably slipped out of one of her meetings to answer my call. "Well, Mr. Moab has cleared his calendar for the entire week, including some rendezvous with Vera."

I asked if Ethan knew why, but he said that he didn't. Apparently, Dunstan Moab had left the California office rather abruptly two days ago to head to the European office here in Italy and had created a logistics nightmare for the operations team. "He was actually set to resume the European rail tour, but with this latest disappearing act, we have no idea what he is going to do," Ethan said. We started wrapping up the call because Ethan had to return to his meeting. "Of course Vera, is on the war path. She says she is stressed out with trying to find a replacement for you. But we both know why she is really pissed." He chuckled.

I giggled back. "Why is that?"

"Hmm, who knows?" Ethan replied playfully. "I've got to go, but we need to catch up."

After hanging up from Ethan, I hobbled over to the window and looked outside. I was tempted to head down to the office since I had only just arrived, but the angry nerve in my ankle felt otherwise. Instead I moved to the tiny desk neatly situated in the corner of the living room and pored over the project I was working on from there. After a while, my ankle began to throb, and I remembered Pete's instructions about keeping the leg elevated. It was then that I spied Dunstan's forgotten iPod on the table.

I reached for the phone, and my heart did a jump of excitement as I heard the line ringing on the other end. I couldn't believe how excited I was at the possibility of speaking with him once more, and when he answered, I almost forgot what I had called for.

"Desti?" he asked after a few seconds had passed and I still hadn't said a word. I could tell that he was moving around because I could hear the exertion in his voice. "Desti, are you okay? Is everything okay? Do you need something?"

"Hello. No, everything is fine, really. I just wanted to let you know that you left your iPod here."

"Oh yes, that's right. Well, maybe you can bring it to lunch— that is, if you still are interested in having lunch with me." He said the last words a bit more softly. I imagined that he was holding his breath, waiting on my reply.

"Yes, of course, no worries. I can bring it then," I replied, now eagerly taking a look at the clock. We had agreed to a late lunch, and it was already after noon.

"How is that ankle of yours? Are you following the good doctor's instructions?" he asked.

"Well, to be truthful, it is really throbbing. I think that I left it hanging too long or that the painkillers are wearing off, or maybe both," I replied. Since breakfast, I had dropped the tough-girl act because he was so easy to talk to, and even though it seemed like we were from two different worlds, when we had interacted, it felt as though we were long-lost friends.

"Okay, well, I thought maybe we could have lunch together up here; would that be okay?" he asked.

"Up where? Where are you?" I asked, confused.

"Here, just above you on the hill, is my home," he replied. "In fact," he continued, "there is more than enough room for you up here. You can stay here if you like so that you can keep off of that ankle of yours. I'll be gone most of the time, but the house is fully equipped with help that you could use."

Just then, I accidentally knocked the cover from the breakfast tray, which clanged noisily to the floor. Hello, clumsiness. This time he laughed out loud, and I imagined his perfect teeth lighting up his even more perfect face. It amused me that "perfect" seemed to be the only word that fit him. The thought of being in close proximity with him overwhelmed me, and I threw caution to the wind, quickly replying without giving a thought to any consequences.

"I think I better get you moved as quickly as possible. After all, it is my fault that you are hobbling around down there on your own. I'll be right down—don't need you doing any more damage to yourself," he said.

I hadn't really unpacked, so by the time Dunstan arrived, I had put a few things together. I had never done anything like this before, and I shivered from excitement at the thought of spending time with Dunstan. When he arrived, he was accompanied by Pete, who looked at me with some measure of concern after inspecting my ankle. I felt faint in the knees as Dunstan moved closer to me, and I almost jumped at the "just out of the shower" freshness that invaded my nostrils. He smelled like soap and shampoo. I quickly snapped my eyes open when I caught myself inhaling his shirt—again. He looked down at me with a slight smile on his lips. I hoped I wasn't drooling. I started hobbling toward the door as Pete grabbed the bag that I had placed on the floor. Unfortunately, one of my wonderful headaches returned, causing me to almost swoon as Dunstan drew near.

"Desti, are you okay?" he said. "Here, please let me carry you to the car."

I put my arm clumsily around him, but once I'd managed the task, the tenseness in his body seemed to release. I felt like I was being carried by air. Whether it was the intoxication of his scent or the thinning air in the hills or my closeness to his body that did it, I couldn't tell, though I suspected it was the latter. I looked back and saw Pete observing our interaction with furrowed brow. He smiled suddenly when we made eye contact and then ushered Dunstan to the door.

Dunstan put me in the back of the car and sat beside me. Pete and my bags occupied the front seats. Pete volunteered to give me a quick tour of the Tuscan countryside after learning how much I was in love with our surroundings, and I accepted the offer. The banter was animated and fun, and I felt more at rest and at ease than I had felt in a long time. In the end Dunstan and I both agreed that Pete should join us for lunch.

We drove through the picturesque village San Gimignano, one of Tuscany's—probably one of Italy's—most iconic regions. I'd always loved Tuscany, and to be in the small village in the heart of Italy's wine country was thrilling. We drove past narrow streets, quaint squares, and centuries-old towers that still retained a medieval air. Eventually, we rounded back to the offices, driving past and up over the hill. Soon we left the main road and approached an imposing, impressive gate that stood almost twenty feet tall. It was fitted to beautifully carved concrete posts with eagles mounted atop.

A crest was engraved into the belly of each eagle, and an intricate pattern at the top of the gate reflected the surrounding foliage. The two sides of the gate swung open, and we passed through, onto a drive lined with trees, whose branches met and formed a natural arc above us. The path rounded shortly and was surrounded by natural woods. The area was heavily wooded and felt secluded, but not in a creepy way. Tall lampposts dotted the path, and I felt as though I was being transported into another world. Beautiful leaves flowered the path, and there was an old-world feel to the surroundings, with fresh, clean air. Soon our destination came into view ahead, nestled into a hill.

My jaw dropped in awe as I took it all in. A waterfall cascaded behind the house, and it looked like it was falling right into the middle of the house. When we disembarked, I would have spun in circles to take it all in if I could have. European-style statues adorned the garden, which was spread across seven terraces next to the home. To one side there were neo-Renaissance gardens built on terraces, with flowerbeds, statues, and fountains - all of it simply stunning. The covered carport was being watched over by a towering statue that I recognized as King Carol. Dunstan hung back as I stood there with my mouth open, taking it all in.

Quietly, he placed his arm around me so that I could ease off the ankle. He asked if I was okay to walk, but before I could answer, he lifted me easily and carefully and walked toward the front of the house. He set me down gently at the door, and in the back of my mind, it registered that he didn't break a sweat whenever he carried me. I turned around and took in the valley below. I couldn't decide which was more impressive: the view from below, from above, or right next to me. Dunstan turned, observing me as I took in the view of the valley below. He remained quiet until I got the courage to face him. He was smiling when I finally got the courage to face him, and he took my arm and slowly led me inside.

Several people who were outside stopped their activities when we walked by. The attention embarrassed me a bit, but I soon forgot as I hopped through the doors. The entry hallway was long and led to expansive French doors that opened to a wonderful courtyard. The wood floors gleamed in the morning sun. I recognized them as macassar ebony, also known as calamander wood, from my last trip to Southeast Asia. Although this wasn't true ebony, it was procured from a related species. The visually striking wood was dark brown to black with orange-gold streaks and contrasted wonderfully with the white-washed walls.

On the right, the sitting room housed leather chairs. I recognized them as Italian-designed Sunpan modern Bugatti chairs, and they flanked two oversized windows that looked more like doors. I had been with Ethan when he sorted the delivery of the chairs two or three years ago. I remembered the price tag and thought that they were pretty pricey for just chairs. The top-grain leather cushions sat on stainless steel legs. They looked comfortable yet almost like a piece of art that one would just sit and observe. Through an entryway on the left was the kitchen. It looked large and comforting with custom walnut floors. I didn't get the opportunity to take much of it in as I became aware of Dunstan's hand on my arm, gently coaxing me along. Dunstan led me around the main entryway and into a guest room. It felt larger than my entire cottage down the hill. There was an oversized couch in front of a fireplace and a four-poster bed that looked too comfortable not to dream in. The shades behind the bed were drawn, and Dunstan fiddled with a small remote in his hand. The blinds opened, and directly behind them, a water feature cascaded beautifully down a rock face. As the blinds opened, I realized that they also let the outside sounds of nature in.

He gave me the remote and quickly ran through the basics. "When all else fails, the panel is on the side of the wall over there—it controls everything that this does. I hope that you'll be okay here." He drew closer to me, and I could feel an intense heat and energy growing between us. He moved a lock of hair that had fallen loose and stared at me for a few seconds, until Pete appeared in the doorway.

Pete's eye twinkled as he eyed the proximity of Dunstan and me and placed my bags near the door. "You pack amazingly light for a girl," he said with a smile, and suddenly the anxiety and nervousness I felt all day disappeared. I felt comfortable around him, and he seemed to be at ease with everyone and everything. He then bounded out of the room, muttering something about some work he needed to finish.

Dunstan turned to me again and, to my surprise, took me by the hand. "Keep off that ankle for a few days; give it some time to heal." I could feel the warmth spreading from my hands to the rest of my body.

He looked to the floor as he continued. "I'm in the room above you, and the stairway is just down the hall. I'm number 7 on the extension here." He pointed to the phone on the bedside table. "I can leave you for a bit to get settled, and when you are ready, we can head off to grab some lunch."

"Oh, no need to give me time," I replied, almost too eagerly. "Besides, I want to see the rest of the house."

When Dunstan looked up, he seemed almost as relieved as I was that we would still be together. Whatever was happening between us was happening quickly and deeply.

Chapter 8

———— ∿∿∿∿∿∿∿ ————

We slowly headed to the terrace on the east side of the house. As we arrived, Pete rounded the corner right behind us, with a broad smile on his face. He reached for me to lean on to him while Dunstan pulled out a chair for me to sit. There was something very familiar about Pete—the way he always seemed happy and how everything and everyone around him seemed to catch that happiness. When I tried to gracefully settle into the chair, the result was more of a plop, and I nearly lost my balance. This drew a faint smile from Pete and a look of concern from Dunstan. Now that we were all sitting so close, I had the opportunity to really look at the two guys who were treating me like a long-lost friend. They seemed very at ease with each other but couldn't be more different, like night and day. Dunstan was dark and mysterious, whereas Pete was a poster boy for Southern California. Dunstan's gray eyes picked up the blue reflection in Pete's. Dunstan's hair was stylishly cut, and Pete's looked as though the wind was his stylist. They were chatting away with each other when lunch arrived a few minutes later. Pretty soon, as we were finishing our food, they turned their attention fully to me.

"Tell us a little about you," Pete said with a grin.

I was quiet for a bit as I contemplated whether or not I should go into the details of my life, or what I remembered of it. I decided I had nothing to lose and so jumped in. "Well, it's a bit of a mouthful," I said. "One for the books." I paused and began again. "I awoke in a hospital several years ago with just snippets of my memory."

Dunstan had set his plate aside and focused his beautiful eyes on me; he hardly blinked as I told my story.

"I was found in Yosemite National Park in California, near the falls. Even though I was pretty traumatized by it all, I can still clearly remember the falls' white foam cascading over what I thought then was a painter's canvas. The image has stuck with me through the years. I was told that I had taken some sort of fall while on the trail. When I came to, a cool spray wisped across my face, interlaced with the scent of the green foliage. The smell of moist soil, stone, and wood, unique to the location, wafted over me and permanently stayed in my nostrils. On the day I awoke, the doctor explained that I was suffering from selective amnesia, meaning some facets of my memory were lost. The skills that I had learned from everyday life were still with me, so he figured that the effects were not long-term."

Pete leaned forward, intrigued with my story. "So you have no recollection of anything before the fall?" he asked.

"No," I replied, swirling my spoon in the remains of the delicious sorbet that had concluded the meal. "At the hospital, I was given my personal effects which they said that they found next to me. It consisted of an old, tattered purse, a bank card, and a rusted pendant with two letter D's intertwined around a rose. A search on the social security card that was in my purse revealed that both my parents had died and that I was eighteen." I shook my head and glanced at Dunstan, who remained silent and transfixed on me.

"The hospital staff questioned me a few times in an attempt to find any living relative, but since they could find none and I had no recollection of anything and I was officially an adult, I was discharged a few days later. The good doctor then advised that I seek some sort of therapy and even suggested a few doctors who specialized in the field. He wished me good luck, and that was it. I stepped into the world with nothing but the tattered purse and gratitude that I was alive, despite the circumstances.

"My first stop was the nearest bank as printed on the card. The address on the account was a post office box, so the bank held no information about my history. I was as much a stranger to them as I was to myself. I withdrew what I felt could last me for a few weeks, checked into a small but clean motel, invested in an inexpensive laptop, and began searching for myself."

"In the following days and nights, as I continued my search for my identity, I came to realize that I had an irrepressible urge to learn. I couldn't understand how come there were no records of an address anywhere. I wasn't on any of the social media sites, I had no high school records, nothing. It was like I just appeared here." I said.

"I did a mock SAT to see if I was educated enough to go after the real thing since I wasn't sure what I knew or how far I had gotten in my studies. I scored in the ninetieth percentile, so I decided to sign up at a local community college to acquire my GED since I wasn't sure that I had one."

I paused upon realizing that I was rattling on and giving more of my story than I had intended to, but it was too late now—both Dunstan and Pete remained quiet, waiting for me to go on. "Believe it or not I was able to complete college through a full scholarship at Pepperdine, and picked up my degrees there. I have to admit, I'm a bit of a nerd, and I'm happy about that! But honestly, it was as if I had this guardian angel watching over me throughout everything that I've been through, helping me out, and making sure that the things I needed to survive were there. Anyway, with that out of the way, I acquired an internship position in the management company of Dream Scape Inc., and the rest is history."

"So you have been on your own all these years?" Dunstan finally asked. He seemed pained and stressed by the idea.

"Well, not completely. I still have irritating headaches that are forever my company. I guess they're from the fall," I replied, trying to lighten the mood. It didn't work because now I had concerned the doctor in Pete.

"Have you ever been back to get a proper check—to see if there is any residual damage?" he asked.

"Every year since then, and there hasn't been a diagnosis yet." I paused, now regretting that I had shared so much because it seemed to have dulled the earlier happy mood. "Come on, guys—lighten up, please; don't feel sorry for me. My experience has made me what I am, and I'm happy with that person and with the results of my hard work. After all, if not for that experience, I wouldn't be sitting with two of the most intriguing people that I will probably ever meet, here in this fantastic place." I looked around, but my eyes lingered on Dunstan. He didn't look away.

"Right, well, lunch is over for me. I have to be on a flight in a few hours," Pete said as he rose. He leaned in to kiss me on the cheek, catching me off-guard, considering that we had only just met. "Now you take it easy on that ankle of yours. I'll see you again pretty soon, I'm sure."

Dunstan reached out to help me to my feet. I took his hand as casually as it was offered. My fingers still trembled slightly though when he tucked them beneath his arm to offer me more support.

Pete nodded and with a smile said, "See ya, Desti." He whistled as he walked away.

"Is he always like that—you know, happy?" I couldn't help but smile as I watched him go. "I feel like I've known him for forever," I said, hobbling slowly along with Dunstan and putting my hand back to my cheek where Pete had pecked me good-bye.

"Yeah, Pete's always been like that." Dunstan put his arm all the way around me so that I had no choice but to lean into him. "His happiness is contagious."

I felt woozy again and chided myself to take control of these feelings that were quickly emerging whenever Dunstan was near. A headache loomed on the horizon, and I wasn't sure I could handle both that and my throbbing ankle.

"Are you okay?" Dunstan asked. "Your ankle—how is it?"

"Well, it still hurts, and unfortunately, I'm feeling a bit of a headache coming on," I replied.

"Well, why don't you head back to your room and get some rest," he said, shortening his stride so that I could keep up. "Maybe we can watch a movie or something when you are up to it later."

"Why, Mr. Moab, are you asking me on a date? I'm not sure that would be appropriate, considering that you are my boss and all," I said playfully.

"I'm sorry." He stopped walking, a worried look creasing his brow. "I'm being too forward. I didn't mean to put you in an uncomfortable situation."

I paused, becoming serious. I needed to let him know that I wasn't interested in being part of the Dunstan-Vera equation. "Look, let me be straight with you," I said. "I don't want to get in between you and Vera."

"Vera?" he asked, gently pulling me by the elbow toward my room again. "Why would you think that there is something happening between Vera and me?"

"Well, the dinners, the morning after your last invitation, I met her coming out of your cabin—I just don't want to be part of a situation," I said.

"Situation? … Oh, that's why! After the train ride, I couldn't understand why you shut down on me. I get it." Dunstan threw back his head and laughed. "There is no situation. Vera and I have been working together on the transition of the company for months now. And as for the night after our dinner together—I left for Tuscany that same evening, and I'm not sure how I could have been two places at once," he said softly. "Believe me, I have no interest in Vera. There is nothing going on."

I shook my head and thought back to all the innuendos Vera had made and the interactions that she had openly talked about and quickly saw how she had twisted everything to her favor.

"I guess Vera was marking her territory." I laughed nervously, still unsure of whether I was making the right decision. I shook my head and decided to go for it. "I'd love to go with you."

Dunstan laughed then, and I couldn't help but wish that later was sooner. The walk back to my room was way too short. Once we arrived, Dunstan exhaled slowly.

He turned me to face him, gently rubbing my arms. "Well, I have to go, and I'm really sorry for any misunderstanding," he said. Then he motioned at my ankle. "For everything."

He opened my door, and I hobbled in. In the next moment, he was gone, and I was alone. It was funny how, in such short space of time, I could already miss him and feel lonely. I sat on the bed and decided to return Ethan's calls, which I had ignored when they came in during lunch. Upon reaching him, I explained that I was now at Dunstan's house and why, and from his hushed tone, I could tell that he was a little more than curious about this.

"Look, Desti, all I'm saying to you … is to be careful up there." Ethan sighed. "If you need me, I'm here," he said reassuringly.

When I finished my call with Ethan, I felt irritated, though I didn't know why. I worked for another few hours and then decided to run the water in the tub and take a soak. Across from the tub, an oversized double-sink vanity reflected the light of the chandelier in the middle of the room. *Who puts a crystal chandelier in a bathroom?* I wondered. When the tub had filled, I hopped over to it, but first

I checked its depth to see if I would drown if I accidentally fell in. Timidly, I stepped in and immersed myself completely in yummy, sudsy water. It did wonders for me, and within minutes, I was incredibly relaxed and felt like I was glowing. An hour later, I made a few more random calls regarding other projects I was working on, and then I lay across the luxurious bedding to check my e-mail. Pretty soon, I fell asleep.

Chapter 9

—⁓ⱽⱽⱽⱽ⌒⌒⌒⌒⌒⌒ⱽⱽⱽⱽ—

Dunstan paced the room impatiently, waiting for Pete. He had to stop himself at least three times from going back to check on Destiny. They were so close to finding a solution to this seven-year process, and he wished he could just stop everything and be with her. He knew that Pete was a bit miffed, but he couldn't help himself. He also knew that despite it all, Pete was also ecstatic to finally be speaking to his long-lost sister once again. They both had been working day and night to find a way to return her, and now they were closer than ever. He recapped the events in his head, and as incredible as everything seemed, he was a part of the reality that was finally unfolding.

Destiny was trapped in this dimension. The accident that had occurred when she accidentally jumped had locked her here. Dunstan with the aid of his father's guilty conscience and deep pockets, had spent years perfecting the jump machine in their dimension while setting up Dream Scape Inc., specifically aimed at finding Destiny and then bringing her home. Upon finding her, they had spent never-ending hours, days and nights trying to figure out a way to bring her back. But finally, Dunstan could stand it no longer and had determined to make contact with her. He had almost lost his mind when she disappeared years earlier, and it was only through Pete that he had been able to pull himself out of the abyss of grief. Now he wasn't sure which was more torturous, not knowing what had happened to her or having her within arm's reach but yet so far away.

Dunstan fiddled with the remote and played his favorite track; Destiny had written it in their dimension when she was a first year studying musical composition and he was a senior studying physics. Dunstan and Pete had been able to jump small objects from one dimension to the other and had celebrated a measure of success a few weeks ago in jumping Destiny's cat Charm. He knew that it was only a matter of time before he would be able to bring her home. He closed his eyes and relived the days of endless conversation, surfing the waves, amazed by her command of the ocean. He then let his mind wander to the lazy summer evenings that they had spent together, his head in her lap as they listened to her music and he helped her to critique her amazing work. He missed her with the same intensity as he had years ago, and the love he had for her had not dissipated over time. In fact it had intensified.

"Dunstan," Pete said quietly, interrupting his memories. Pete had entered silently, and Dunstan was so engrossed in his thoughts of Destiny that he hadn't noticed his arrival.

"I know what you're going to say, Pete, but doesn't it feel wonderful to have her back? Talking to her, being with her—we are so close; maybe this will all help somehow," Dunstan said.

"Well," Pete said, "what I was going to say is that you were absolutely right about making contact. I was wrong; this was a good idea."

Dunstan could tell that Pete was beginning to get emotional. But why wouldn't he? Downstairs in one of the guest bedrooms was the only living relative Pete had left.

"So you aren't pissed off?" Dunstan asked.

"No, I'm not. But right now, you need to cross over. You know the drill—you've been away too long as it is. We don't want to disrupt your balance," Pete replied.

Dunstan knew that Pete was right. Pete remained in the room while Dunstan took to his bed. Lately, he'd found that in order to get into the deep sleep he needed, he had to rely on a sleep agent that Pete administered. The longest any of them had stayed in this dimension was just about seven consecutive days. Dunstan sometimes would go for days without rejuvenating because he never reached the REM sleep he needed to reach in order to complete the process. In his dimension they jumped in a very controlled environment. The first "self" attached itself to the consciousness of the second self, while the body physically remained in its respective dimension. This was what had gone wrong when Destiny accidentally jumped. She somehow had been able to jump mind and body altogether, and they were only now able to replicate the events of that fateful day even in small ways. Part of the issue was that seven days here aged the body in his dimension by about fourteen years—about two years per day—and on their side they had to stay in the rejuvenation chamber for seven hours to reverse the effects of the jump. Destiny's jump had fueled a violent reaction in her brain, erasing her memories of the first dimension. It was this that they were working to rectify, to ensure that such a catastrophe would never reoccur.

It seemed to be an almost impossible task, but years ago, both he and Pete had decided to find the solution, at any cost. And now they were here with her, and if he wasn't mistaken, she was falling for him again. At least he hoped so. This was his definition of soul mates. Despite circumstance, true soul mates were never separated—this was the belief that had kept him through the years.

A few minutes after falling asleep, Dunstan awoke in his dimension. He got up and returned Ayala's grin.

"She's going to be home soon—I can feel it!" Ayala said in her ever-bubbly, ever-optimistic Aussie accent. "Let's get you young again," she said, motioning to Dunstan's graying temples.

Over the years, Ayala had dedicated her study of medicine and cell science to perfecting the rejuvenation chamber. Ayala and Pete had met just around the same time that he and Destiny had, and they had been together ever since. She and Pete had gotten married in a small but romantic ceremony a few years ago, but they were just as loopy-eyed as new lovers each time they saw each other. Ayala had formed a strong sisterly bond with Destiny before the accidental jump, and she too was aching to be reunited with Destiny soon.

Dunstan kissed Ayala lightly on the cheek and went over to the rejuvenation chamber to begin his seven-and-a-half-hour nap. He had tucked a small photo of him and Destiny, from when they were teenagers, in the folds the plush material of the chamber, and it was this image that remained stamped on his brain when he fell asleep a few minutes later.

Just around eight in the evening, Dunstan tapped lightly on Destiny's door. She opened the door looking refreshed and relaxed. She was wearing a peach sweater that brought out the color in her cheeks beautifully, and even though he could tell that she was still in pain, she seemed genuinely delighted to see him. He couldn't help but grin widely at the sight of her. Her eyes were pools of hazel and chocolate that effortlessly mesmerized him, and she had long, lustrous lashes the color of midnight, which she blinked almost constantly. Her skin shone healthily, and she had let down her hair, which fell loosely over her shoulders into slack curls.

Her lips were like a frozen rose, and he longed to recall the texture of them. She smiled brightly at him, and the soft glow from the dimmed lights made her even more beautiful than he remembered. He returned the smile and said tenderly, "You look amazing, Desti."

"Thank you, Dunstan," she replied, smiling shyly and sweetly.

"I thought that maybe we could watch a movie, but I haven't eaten as yet, and I'm starving. Have you eaten?" he asked.

"Well, actually I haven't," she said.

"Okay, that's great; let me cook for you."

"How about we do that together?" she answered, tucking her hand easily under his arm to ease the weight off her ankle.

The house was quiet for the most part because Dunstan had given everyone the night off. As they walked toward the kitchen, he watched Destiny take in every inch of the house.

"This is a fantastic house," she said in the kitchen, gesturing around and above her. "It has a silent grandeur, but it isn't too overpowering." Her eyes were wide and bright as she ran her fingers across the Carrara marble countertops. The oversized leaded glass windows were so tall that they almost touched the brick-and-wood ceiling. Next to one window was a Lacanche range with a fireback, and a zinc-and-steel hood that looked custom-designed hovered over the eleven burners. Destiny loved kitchens and wished she had more time to spend in them—and this one was fantastic. The island provided an expansive counter space and was surrounded by leather and stainless steel bar stools. Destiny hopped over to one, and pretty soon the room was filled with the delicious aromas of simmering sauces and cheesy pasta.

Dunstan had elevated Destiny's leg so that she could work on the salad and toasted garlic bread. He poured her a glass of wine, which was light and fruity.

"This is delicious," she said as she set down her wine glass.

Dunstan grinned. "I knew you would like it." In a few minutes he brought a plate in front of her encouraging her to dig in. He set his plate next to hers, and she obeyed easily as the smell of melted cheese filled her nostrils. The food was delicious, and the conversation between them flowed easily.

"You know, Dunstan," Destiny said in between chews, "I hope that you don't think this is some sort of frivolous come-on, but it feels really good to be around you. It feels as though I've known you for a really long time."

Dunstan only nodded his head and smiled.

They spent the evening talking about everything. Dunstan told her about his dad and his life in Europe, but he seemed more interested in learning as much as possible about her and how she had survived after her accident and memory loss. He was lovable and adorable, as well as extremely intelligent, and he was just so wonderful to be around. He seemed so interested in her life and the things she had experienced. He was impressed at with accomplishments, and she beamed inwardly to hear his accolades. As Destiny finished her last bite, Dunstan reached to take her plate away. He then returned and helped her to the couch in front of the large fireplace in the den.

He paused close to her face and moved a tendril behind her ear. "So are you okay up here?"

Destiny nodded and wet her lips, hardly breathing. As he slowly, forcibly pulled himself away, he was sure that she could hear the distinct thudding of his heart against her chest. A moment later, he was bustling around in the kitchen as she sank into the cushion, pulling the warm blanket closer around her. The den looked out toward the valley below, and the twinkling lights in the distance set a romantic ambience. Dunstan was enjoying himself thoroughly and didn't want the evening to end.

He returned with the most delicious drink she had ever seen. "It's a chocolatini," he said. "And it's light on the vodka. I hope that you like it."

Destiny took a sip and melted almost immediately. "It's fantastic! Absolutely fantastic."

Dunstan beamed and returned to the couch beside her, nursing a beverage of his own. He repositioned the pillows around her and then fiddled with the remote to start the massive fireplace that took up one side of the wall. As the night had worn on, the house had gotten chillier, and the fireplace was welcoming and comforting. He put on some soothing music, and once again they began chatting away about everything and anything.

After a while, Dunstan's words started to fade as the music seemed to take over their conversation. "Who is this?" she asked. "That is so wonderful." Destiny was entranced by the melody. She closed her eyes and fell into a lull as the notes filled her ears. She sank deeper into the cushions, and Dunstan drew closer to her.

"I know the composer," he finally said. "She went to school with Pete and me."

Destiny touched her temples as the headache that had dulled in the last few hours returned suddenly with full force.

"Headache?" Dunstan asked.

"Yeah, I took some of Pete's meds though, so I'm sure it will go away," she replied absently, still entranced by the music surrounding them. Her eyes closed slowly as she turned her body toward Dunstan. He put his arm around her, and she rested her head on his shoulder.

He pulled the blanket around them, and as she dozed, he thought of how quickly things were moving between the two of them. He brushed her hair back from her face and kissed her lightly and tenderly on the forehead, and pretty soon he too fell asleep.

Destiny dreamt about Dunstan. It was a long and sweet dream—they were at a beach somewhere in the Pacific, diving, looking at life on a reef. They held hands as they swam around the reef. In her dream she felt exhilarated by the electricity flowing between them. She could see the smile in his eyes as he glanced over at her, playfully shooing a school of turquoise and neon-blue fish in her direction. His hair was longer, but his beautiful gray eyes were the same. They zipped around the reef and played hide-and-seek with each other. They collected shells from the reef before heading back to the surface.

They swam to a docked boat, and as soon as they resurfaced, Dunstan threw his mask into the boat and reached for her. He gently removed her mask and touched her face before fiercely kissing her. He took her breath away as he supported them both in the unbelievably blue water. He then released her and hoisted her into the boat. He was smiling at her, and her heart was filled with a happiness that she couldn't describe. Throughout the dream, she could hear every word Dunstan said without actually seeing his lips move.

She awoke with a start on the couch in front of the warm fire. Dunstan lay beneath her, and his deep, slow breathing indicated he was asleep too. His arm was draped lightly around her waist, and even in his sleep, he seemed to draw her back to him. She watched him in the flickering fire for a few moments before dozing off again, feeling comforted and warm and safe.

Chapter 10

—〰◦◦✺✺✺◦◦〰—

I awoke the next morning just as the sun was peeking over the horizon. I rose to one elbow and studied the face of the sleeping man beside me. It was as if an artist had created him from a stencil, skillfully perfecting each stroke and line of his face. I traced the shape of his eyes and couldn't resist touching the side of his face to make sure that he was indeed real and lying right beside me. Pretty soon, his eyes fluttered open, and try as I might, I couldn't look away from his gaze. His eyes were almost a transparent gray, and every time I caught sight of them, I felt lost. His hair was tousled, but he was gorgeous just the same.

"Good morning," he said softly. Just as he was drawing me closer to him, a furry mass of tail and tongue jumped on us, showering us with a thousand kisses. The golden retriever placed her paws on the couch beside us, happily wagging her tail, as Dunstan tousled her head. The moment gone, I chuckled at the sight of Dunstan receiving such deep canine affection.

"Boxie, there you are. How is my girl?" Dunstan said into her fur. "How are you feeling? Where is Ayala?"

Just then Pete bounded into the room and smiled at us as we tried to extricate ourselves from blankets and fur. I righted myself just before a blonde woman rounded the corner after Pete. Boxie left Dunstan and went to her side, showering her and Pete with affection too.

"Hi there," the woman said, stooping to hug Boxie.

"Desti, this is my wife Ayala," said Pete. Ayala rose and moved to my side. Her eyes seemed misty, and her hand trembled slightly as she greeted me. Boxie nudged Ayala once again, as if upset that her petting time had been interrupted, and Ayala bent to fully embrace the affectionate dog.

"Pete has told me all about you. You have no idea how happy I am to meet you. Pete hasn't quite shut up since meeting you." She turned away, seemingly emotional.

"Hey, I remember you! We met at the pet rescue. I dropped a kitten off a few weeks ago. Wow, small world! How is he?" I asked.

"Oh yes, small world indeed!" she replied, exchanging a quick glance with Dunstan. "Oh, he is fine—we haven't placed him yet, but he is quite a character." She spun around and continued, "I'm glad you are here. The boys, as I call them—they live such hard lives. I mean, there are things that affect them that they have to think about all the time, that we take for granted. They have no freedom, you know, to live." She shrugged her shoulders. "But today, Pete is happy, and Dunstan is definitely happy, and maybe things will work out after all."

I was a bit confused by Ayala's words, which carried an undertone of something more serious than a casual meet-and-greet, but all was soon forgotten among clanging plates, popping toast, and the aroma of fresh coffee.

"How is that ankle of yours coming along?" Ayala asked, reaching out once more to take me by the arm. Ayala continued chatting away with me, almost oblivious to the men.

For reasons unexplainable, I liked Ayala instantly. She was warm and energetic, and she and Pete seemed to match. Her laughter was contagious, and it filled the room with warmth.

After reassuring everyone that my ankle was doing much better, I excused myself from the wonderful breakfast we had shared. The time had flown by amid the banter, and suddenly I felt the need to process all that had happened so far. Dunstan rose and took me by the arm as we moved through the hallways back to my room. It was unseasonably warm in the house today, and Dunstan suggested that we take advantage of the sunny day with lunch in the village. I accepted, thrilled at the opportunity to see him again soon, and we continued through the house in comfortable silence. The electricity between us intensified with each step, and I almost held my breath when we reached my door. Dunstan seemed to be searching for words at first, but in the end he merely kissed me on the cheek and wished me a good day.

As he headed back to the others, Dunstan knew that he needed to spend more time working on his side to analyze everything that they had learned so far. He couldn't put it off any longer, but each time he was away from Destiny, he was torn up by the separation. He and Pete would have to discuss Destiny's headaches and their probable cause, and this had thrown a wrench in their plan to get her home. No one had factored in possible health risks outside of rejuvenation, which was a huge enough risk on its own. Now a whole series of tests and theorizing had commenced. Pete still thought that she wasn't yet ready to hear the full details of who she was and where she came from; Dunstan didn't agree.

He knew his irritation at the delay was selfish, and he understood Pete's concern. They'd had another huge fight earlier when Dunstan announced that he was going to try to explain the entire process and what had happened to her. Pete had argued that he would rather just have her here than put her through any more risk or pain, but Dunstan had countered that this wasn't their decision to make.

Joining the fray, Ayala had taken his side against Pete's, and a whole new argument fueled by Ayala's "down under" temper had ensued. Dunstan had then heard the faint meow before seeing it—and there was Charm, a.k.a. "Mr. Kitty," trailing behind Ayala and Pete.

"I'm sorry—I couldn't help it," Ayala had said. "But I figured that this would be a great surprise. After all, he is her cat." And that had broken the argument as angry voices were replaced with laughter.

I closed the door behind me and felt the familiar traces of dull pain knocking at my temple. I headed straight to the shower and let the invigorating jet streams soothe some of the pain away. When I got out of the shower, I heard a gentle nudge against my door, and as I opened it slightly, a beautiful mound of golden fur pushed her way inside, her silver collar clanging in beat to the movement of her happily wagging tail. Boxie made herself at home on the rug on the floor and watched me with intelligent eyes as I limped around to get dressed. In truth my ankle was feeling about 90 percent better; whatever Pete had given me seemed to be accelerating the healing process.

I had turned the little desk in the corner of the room into a workstation and was able to drag over a poof on which to prop my ankle. Deciding to play some music, I fiddled with the remote and was surprised at what came through the speakers. The song was the same one that Dunstan had played the night before, except in this version, it was being played by some grand orchestra and remixed with modern music. It was captivating and fun at the same time. I could almost see and feel the musicians playing and watch the instruments following instructions; it was beautiful. I pressed repeat and found pretty soon that I was humming softly, surprised that I was able to pick up the melody so fast. I then delved into my work, occasionally pausing to smile at the twitching dog beside me, who was obviously dreaming of supersized Milk-Bones and bacon.

Shortly before twelve-thirty, there was a tap on the door. I answered and ushered Ayala in—she was on the hunt for Boxie.

"There you are," she said, petting the dog, who now stretched and yawned lazily. Ayala looked at me and laughed before returning her gaze to Boxie. "So you've been locked away for the past few hours with Desti," she said, reaching to tousle the stretching dog's hair again. I noticed Ayala's use of my pet name, which again I didn't recall ever mentioning. Ayala stood and shook some of Boxie's fur from her hands and said, "Dunstan has had to leave and didn't want to disturb you. Would you like to join Pete and me for a quick bite? We're heading down to our favorite little place back in town."

"Sure," I replied, a bit disappointed that I would not get to see Dunstan as soon as I'd hoped, but happy to spend some more time with my new friends. I had led such a lonely life, and besides Ethan, there was really no one else. It was nice to have a girlfriend for a change.

"Great! Let's meet out front in half an hour or so; can you make it on your own?" Ayala asked.

"Yeah, I'm doing so much better," I replied.

"Well, don't get all better too soon; we *all* like having you around." She smiled with a slight twinkle in her eye before leaving with Boxie in tow.

I decided to spend some time exploring the gardens before my lunch date with Pete and Ayala. I wandered slowly around the outside and was especially awed by the landscaping, which featured fountains, urns, and stairways, guarding lions, marble paths, and other decorative pieces. I also got an opportunity to briefly peek into a couple of the rooms on the lower level, and I found that they were even more of a wonder than the luxurious gardens. I especially loved the music room and its sculpted wooden paneling and stained-glass windows. I was enthralled by a few pieces of European art, and the grand piano in the center of the room was polished so well that it reflected the Murano crystal chandelier hanging above it.

I closed the double doors almost reverently behind me and moved to the piano tentatively. Something began stirring deep within me, and I had the urge to stroke each key, which was funny to me because as far as I knew, I had never played a piano in my life. I moved over to the expansive music collection, and my eyes went straight to the center of the shelf, which displayed a simple yet noticeable glass case containing twenty discs. I opened the case and reached for one titled "Gray Skies" and popped it into the player. I recognized it instantly as the piece that Dunstan had played the night before and that I had listened to in my room. I listened to the entire track and found that I could pick up subtle differences in this version. This one felt more vibrant—unpolished yet perfect somehow. I stayed there for a while, evaluating the emotions now surfacing, and surprised myself when I felt tears forming in the corners of my eyes. I replaced the disc and headed back to meet the others.

When I first got outside, Pete was waiting patiently, casually leaning against the car with the engine running. His smile was replaced with a look of concern as he moved toward me instantly, almost as if he could feel what I was feeling.

"Destiny, are you okay?" he asked gently.

"I am," I replied, but I found myself rattling off my experience in the music room. "I don't understand why I felt so affected by the music," I concluded.

Pete remained quiet and offered no explanation. Ayala bounded into the car a few seconds later, and soon we were off. Ayala's bubbly mood pretty soon erased any traces of my sadness as she vividly and enthusiastically described her and Pete's life while we headed toward town.

I learned that Ayala was Australian and had met both Pete and Dunstan at school on a break while surfing the waves in California. Pete added how determined she was to claim him from the moment they met—but, he said with a chuckle, he didn't mind. As we drove through the countryside, I was captivated by the beautiful scenery that whizzed by. Lunch was fun and animated, and the camaraderie between the three of us was great, but every now and then, I could feel Pete silently observing me as he let Ayala chatter on about everything under the sun. By the end of the lunch, I felt like they were a part of my life in some way.

When we returned to the house, Dunstan greeted us with a warm smile, and Boxie ran to me the instant I alighted from the car.

"Hey!" Ayala protested as Boxie ignored her and placed her head on my leg. Dunstan laughed out loud. He helped me from the car, but by now I could put my foot fully on the ground. Pete and Ayala watched us walk into the house with smiles and then left.

Dunstan and I spent an hour or so in the gardens. He tentatively held my hand as we walked along the paths, with Dunstan naming practically every flower in the garden and its symbolic meaning, to my delight. Eventually, he led me back to my room because I had to finish the project I was working on. He told me that he was leaving for Milan early in the morning but that he would be back the day after.

"There is a charity event coming up this weekend. I would love for you to accompany me," Dunstan said, taking my hand in his.

"Why, Mr. Moab, are you asking me on a date?" I asked for the second time, a wide smile on my face.

"Why, Miss Tallum, I believe I am." He opened my door and smiled sweetly before moving aside to let me in.

I gasped when I saw the little mass of fur sleeping deeply on his back in the middle of the bed. It was the kitten I had rescued in Milan.

"The shelter called him Charm," Dunstan said.

"How on earth did you get this done?" I asked as I ran to the bed and scooped up the little kitten, who seemed unbothered by the interruption of his rest, purring as he woke up.

"I've got connections," Dunstan replied simply. Boxie pushed her way in and whined upon eyeing her new competition, and we both laughed. Dunstan followed me into the room, visibly amused by the reunion. Charm pawed my cheek lightly as he had done in the train, climbed to my shoulder, and wrapped his long tail around my neck. Dunstan and I both laughed again.

He took my hand and said, "You don't have to be alone anymore, Destiny."

I reached for him and kissed his cheek. "I'm starting to feel very wanted," I replied.

Dunstan smiled and left, whistling the beautiful tune that we had listened to the night before.

Chapter 11

T he next two days that Dunstan was away seemed to fly by, and by midafternoon on the day of the event, I had hitched a quick ride back to my cottage with Ayala to find something to wear to it. As I unlocked the door and entered, I spotted a white box perched on the table. Ayala saw it too and smiled.

"What's this?" I asked, quickly slipping the red ribbon tied around it. Ayala continued smiling as I gingerly opened it. Inside lay the most beautiful gown I had ever seen.

"Are you serious?" I said with a laugh. "I feel like I'm in a movie or something." I picked up the card inside the box and recognized Dunstan's handwriting on the envelope.

"Well, I'll leave you to it, and I'll see you in a few hours," Ayala said, filling the room with her laughter. Before I could say anything else, she bounded out the door.

I opened the card, which simply said, "You are definitely wanted."

My eyes moistened as I pulled the dress out of the box. It was a beautiful ivory gown with a silk chiffon sweetheart neckline. Draped with a crystal tulle capelet, it was beautiful and simply angelic. I tried it on immediately, and although it was delicate, the long slit in the front showed enough leg to make the overall look sexy and alluring. I was glad that my ankle was feeling better as

I twirled around, checking myself out in the mirror. The dress hugged and draped over all the right places; it was a perfect fit.

A few hours later, as I pinned up the last strands of my hair, I spied myself in the mirror, and even I had to chuckle at the fact that I seemed to be glowing. I told myself that it was the sparkly crystals in the dress, but really, I knew that this was the effect of being with Dunstan and being in his world. Suddenly I was nervous, anticipating his reaction upon seeing me after the short break away.

When I opened the door, and he stopped in mid-greeting, I wasn't sure how to read his face. I smoothed the front of my dress, and he came forward to take my hand.

He was dressed in an off-white shirt with a matching blazer. The clothes fit his frame the way a tailored outfit did. He was breathtaking, and my face showed it. I was entranced by his beauty, and I couldn't seem to tear my eyes away from him.

"You are beautiful—absolutely perfect," he said, his eyes glistening as he enveloped me in his gaze.

We walked to the car, and Ayala hugged me gently, smoothing a tendril of my hair. Pete only nodded in appreciation, but his smile was bright enough to make me laugh out loud. In the ride down, Dunstan sat close to me, his fingers interlaced with mine. As we approached, I noticed that the building was ablaze with lights and music, and cars were already parked neatly at the side of the building.

We stepped up to the entry doors, and I was happy, giddy, and self-conscious as people literally parted for us to enter.

"Dunstan, ever notice the effect that you have on people? They seem to keep an almost reverent distance from you," I whispered as we entered.

"Not everyone," he replied. "I've run into a few that keep trying to knock me over." He laughed. I was smiling at the thought of our encounters so far when he added, "And there are some that have literally knocked me off my feet."

I was thrilled at his words, but before I could digest them, we had entered the main room where the event was taking place. There were about a hundred people there, which meant that a logistics team was somewhere in the wings, planning and working the event. Indeed, when I looked around, I spotted Vera, quietly but forcefully whispering commands into her miniscule earpiece, mostly hidden by her long blonde hair. She nodded imperceptibly as she passed us, and I wondered, as her eyes passed over my arm tucked securely in the arm of Dunstan, what rumor was sure to explode later. But I was bubbling with happiness, and nothing would change that tonight.

We milled around the room, and some people I recognized; others I did not. Dunstan introduced me as Desti to many of the persons who made their way to meet him, and I stood quietly by in awe as he casually advised senators while mingling with the super powerful and uber-rich. He did so with charm and humble elegance that was appealing, and I wanted nothing more than to be there, just silently listening. He escorted me to a seat in the corner almost obscured by a large planter made of coral stone and embroidered with gold, strategically placed to separate the table from the rest of the guests. It was set for two, and I noticed that Pete and Ayala had taken residence at the front of the room.

Amid all the banter and clattering plates and cutlery, my heart thudded against my chest, and in my ears the sound was deafening. Dunstan sat opposite me and smiled sweetly. His eyes seemed to darken, and his face seemed to become even more perfect, if that was possible. A smartly dressed waiter approached us and set the oversized tray on the serving table behind us. To my surprise, throughout the meal, my favorite dishes came out, as if someone knew my fetish for bruschetta, rack of lamb, and crème brûlée. Throughout the meal, it was as if Dunstan and I were alone together. We described people and places we had met and seen. One of his favorite places in all his travels was in the Caribbean, the island of

Barbados. He commented on the friendliness of the people there, the wonderful beaches, and their local rum. He described the water as so blue, everything around or on it reflected a blue hue. But on the top of his list was his home here. He loved the trails and waterfalls, and when there was no one else up there, a peacefulness overtook him that could not be replaced by anything else.

Shortly before 2:00 a.m., with Dunstan at the wheel, we headed back up the hillside. Ayala dozed lightly on Pete's shoulder, and I couldn't help but feel warmed by their feelings for each other. I was a little tired, but I didn't want the night to end. It was chilly outside, but I paid no attention to that. I wanted to spend more time with Dunstan and had to practically shake myself to stop from begging him to stay with me a little longer.

When we arrived, Pete gently scooped Ayala, who was now completely out, from the car as if she were a feather and nodded good night to us. I decided to go for it.

"Sleepy?" I asked Dunstan.

"Not in the least," he said, to my delight.

I hadn't gotten the time to really explore the upper floors of the house, and I was ecstatic when he offered to give me a grand tour. The house had six bedrooms, seven and a half bathrooms, two entertainment rooms, a pool and billiards room, and an ultra-modern office, in addition to the rooms that I had already seen. On the west side of the house on the top floor was an indoor infinity pool, designed to look as though it were running right off the side of the house and in essence off the side of the hill. The house was wedged in the cliff, and the deck was totally encased in glass. The glass could be rolled back remotely, however, to allow the rays of warm summer to penetrate. I also noticed that the ultimate sound system was installed throughout the house. As we passed by Dunstan's room—my favorite room in the house—I heard that familiar beautiful melody softly playing. His room opened out to the terrace with the pool.

"What is it with this tune? It plays everywhere here, and though I am certain that I know it, I just can't seem to place it."

Dunstan paused and seemed to choose his words carefully. "Well, my friend who wrote it ... she was—is—a very talented musician. She wrote symphonies as easily as we dream." He looked wistfully around the room before settling his eyes on me. "This was her last piece."

"I can see why you like it. It's beautiful," I replied, surprising myself with the pang of jealousy I felt at his words.

He paused then, took my hand, and led me out to the terrace. We looked across the treetops, which were now losing their bright autumn hue to the growing coldness.

"Desti, I'm really sorry to hear what you've been through."

I was taken aback by his concern and the effect that my recounting of my past seemed to have on him. I reached for him and placed my hand on his cheek. The moon reflected pools of silver light in his eyes. I felt incredibly drawn to him. I watched him closely while he seemed to be trying to compose himself.

"I wish that I could take back everything that has happened to you," he said. Dunstan rose and walked over to the edge of the infinity pool at the western corner of the terrace. I went over to him and touched his shoulders, which seemed to sag under my touch.

"Is something wrong?" I asked.

He waited for a bit before turning around to face me. He slowly twirled me around like we were in a romantic waltz. Finally, he pulled me close to him and trapped me in his gaze. "No. You are absolutely beautiful and perfect," he said softly. "I'm so glad that I've finally found you." He placed both his hands at the sides of my face. He drew closer to me, and I immediately became immersed in pools of silver light. I looked into his eyes and felt an ease and familiarity that I couldn't explain. My eyes traced every crease of his brow, memorizing everything that I could in case I awoke and realized that this was just a dream. The racing of my pulse, however, reminded me that this was as real as I could ever feel. My knees shook when he gently pressed his lips on mine. He broke away suddenly, as if he too felt the jolt of electricity that I felt buzzing around me, his eyes searching for something. He brought me toward him once again, gently at first and then hungrily, as if finally satisfying a need he'd felt for a very long time.

There was nothing I could do but melt in his arms, overpowered by emotion. At first I timidly placed my arms around his neck, but then something took over, and I wanted more. Surprisingly, a few tears welled up. I couldn't explain the rally of emotions hitting me all at once. I couldn't get enough of him and leaned into him as much as I could; I needed to feel him all around me, all at once.

"There is so much that you need to know," he said softly as he finally pulled away gently. But I couldn't help myself—I pulled him toward me once more.

His lips were soft but persistent as he explored every facet within me with his kiss. My mind felt like it would explode as fiery darts consumed me deep within. An overwhelming feeling of ecstasy caroused through my veins. He responded to my intensity by drawing me even closer to him, and by the time we separated, we were both out of breath. He drew me closer once again and held me tenderly, before kissing me on my forehead sweetly.

Dunstan took my hand, and we walked to the other side of the terrace, where we sank into the plush seating. We remained close together and talked about anything and everything until the sun came up. Throughout our time together, my head pounded, but I was too giddy with happiness to care. Dunstan became worried when he saw me absently massage my temples, but I brushed him off by kissing his fingertips.

He walked me back to my room shortly after 5:00 a.m., and I opened the blinds to catch a glimpse of the waking sun. Sleep was creeping in, and I had to oblige. Just after watching the sun tiptoe over the horizon, I fell asleep, happy and smiling, my lips and skin still tingling from the million butterfly kisses we'd shared as we talked about random thoughts.

The house was quiet when I ventured out of my room a few hours later. I headed to the kitchen to appease my rumbling tummy. In the center of the immense granite island lay a single red rose, resting on an envelope. I pulled out the tiny note inside.

"The First Kiss"
The first meeting of questioning lips
The caught breath as soft muscles meet and explore timidly
Passion intensifies
A thousand thoughts gyrate to the pulsating rhythm of an accelerated heartbeat
Knees weakened, hands trembling
Bodies interlocked, finding support in each other
Playful butterflies across the waistline
Play hide-and-go-seek with chills in the spine
Chills are replaced by growing warmth
Morphing into intense heat
Closed eyelids see blinding light
Lips part, but the fantasy goes on

After the poem, Dunstan added how much he was looking forward to seeing me again soon. I thought of how romantic an actual handwritten note was in today's world of communicating through electronic devices. Dunstan had an old-world feel about him that I absolutely adored. It almost seemed like he belonged to another place and time, and the more time I spent with him, the more I felt like I was a part of that world.

Chapter 12

—◦◦◦◦◦◦◦◦—

Dunstan left Italy the next day on business, which gave me time to get back to my cottage and back to work. My ankle hurt only slightly and only if I stood too long, and I didn't want to slack on my work ethic just because things were happening between us. On my first day back, the office felt hushed, the mood charged, and I knew it was because of the event over the weekend. Dunstan had never been accompanied to any major corporate events by a female companion, so our pairing that night was news around the water cooler. I was prepared for that, however, and simply smiled when I entered, offering no explanation and not acting any different than I had before.

I wasn't hiding what was developing between us, but I wasn't going to offer up any juicy details either. Indeed, I couldn't hide it even if I wanted to because on my desk lay another rose, with another one appearing every day for an entire week. Thankfully, the people I worked with didn't treat me any differently and were as polite and professional as when I'd first arrived.

The upcoming weekend was going to be a long one, and I looked forward to Dunstan's return. Unfortunately, Dunstan's trip had been extended, meaning he would be gone for a second week, but he had called me every day since our first real date.

As I got home on the evening that he was to return, I had a strange sense of not being alone. I turned on all the lights in the house and searched room by room, even looking under the bed, which I did with a chuckle. Just then my phone rang. It was Dunstan.

"Desti, how are you this evening?" he asked, brightening my evening immediately with just the sound of his voice.

"I'm doing great ... just a bit paranoid," I said. I went on to explain the strange feeling I had.

"You probably aren't alone. This is why I'm calling. I was at a press conference yesterday evening, and I might have let something slip about us. The paparazzi will be on the loose, and they have probably set up shop nearby. Your space may be invaded soon. I'm sorry."

I peeked outside but saw no one. But the eerie feeling didn't leave.

"I'll send Pete down for you," Dunstan said, "and I should get there in about an hour or two."

"Okay," I said. "I'll see you soon."

Pete arrived about twenty minutes later, and his sense of humor was so infectious that I forgot about the creepy feeling and was in stitches as soon as we drove off. When we arrived at the house, as I was alighting from the car, my phone fell to ground. Pete grabbed it for me and handed it over, and we went inside to await Dunstan's arrival.

The house smelled wonderful, which meant that a fantastic dinner was in the making, and sure enough, there was Ayala bustling away in the kitchen, amid pots and pans, when we entered. Pete went to help her, and although I offered to as well, I could hardly concentrate from the excitement of seeing Dunstan once more. I heard Dunstan arriving just about an hour later, and Boxie disappeared and headed to the door. I excused myself politely and walked out of the kitchen. Once I was out of sight, I practically raced Boxie to the door. Dunstan was taking his bags from the trunk when I arrived. He turned to face me, and even though I could see that he was tired, he was still as gorgeous as he'd been on the morning after we fell asleep by the fireplace.

"Hi," I said.

He scooped me up into his arms and planted a long, sweet kiss on me, balancing his bags in one hand and me in the other without effort. "I've missed you, Miss Tallum."

"And I, you," I replied.

He set his bags down so that he could fully envelop me with another kiss. I was breathless when we parted. We went inside and greeted the others.

We enjoyed a wonderful dinner that evening, and I couldn't shake the feeling of familiarity as I looked at each of their glowing, beautiful faces. After the meal, Dunstan drove me home. We walked in silence to the front door of my cottage, and before I could say anything, his lips were on mine, soft and sweet. I wanted him so much right there and then and was about to tell him so when he pulled away, as if sensing what I was feeling. He looked into my eyes for a long time and then gently kissed my forehead.

"It feels so good to be here with you," he began softly. Just then, there was a rustle in the brush behind us, and someone ran off into the night. Dunstan spun around and pulled me back into the car and then sped off down the road behind the running figure, who left the road and crossed over into the wooded area. Dunstan called Pete while maneuvering down the winding road back to the offices. Unfortunately, we lost the person, and Dunstan was visibly upset when Pete drove up.

"It must be the press. You know how it is," Pete said to his friend.

"They were outside of her house. We need more security up here," Dunstan said, slamming his fist on to the hood of the car.

"We can't really secure her where she is. The property line is unbounded; that's why we chose it," Pete said. "But the house is fully secure—the only option would be to have her move up there." They both turned and looked at me.

I shook my head with a smile. "Thanks, guys, but it was one photographer. How harmful can he be?"

"You have no idea," Dunstan answered.

The next morning, sitting in my office, I finally understood exactly why Dunstan had made such a big deal. Plastered across the Internet and gossip magazines were photos of me and Pete and then another of me and Dunstan. The first photo had been taken when Pete reached to hand me my phone outside the car. The photographer had snapped the shot exactly when Pete's face was near my leg as he bent to retrieve my phone. The second was of me and Dunstan in an embrace. The headlines basically insinuated that I was having an affair with both Dunstan and Pete. I shook my head in disbelief as I read some of the tabloids taking it even further, saying that this was something I did on a regular basis; one of them claimed that an inside source had told the tabloid this was the reason I had gotten the job heading up the Italian office. I closed my laptop, figuring that the stories were bound to become more ridiculous if I kept on reading. Then there was a knock on my door.

I got up to answer it, still numb from what I had just read. I was pleasantly surprised to see Dunstan standing on the other side.

"Hi, come on in," I said, ushering him in. I peeked outside the door and saw that the usual banter on the floor had evaporated; it felt like everyone was waiting with bated breath.

"I guess you've seen the papers today," Dunstan said, his gray eyes turning almost black.

"Nah, not at all," I said with a giggle. "Seriously, the lengths people will go to make headlines."

"I'm really sorry about all this—we've set up a conference for this afternoon to address this."

"I don't think that you should," I said. "I mean, what are you going to say? That wasn't Pete and me in the picture? Or me and you? You can try to explain that he was just handing me my phone, but we'll probably be scoffed at and just fan even more flames."

Dunstan cocked his head to one side, clearly not understanding where I was taking this. I walked back to my chair and sat, placing my hand on the closed laptop.

"I say let them have their story. Sooner or later, the general public will get over it and take the story for what it really is—fabricated gossip. If you talk to them, then we will forever be in a tug-of-war, with the truth as the rope. After a while, we might even eventually hang ourselves."

Dunstan laughed at my analogy, and I joined him after a moment.

"I say we go somewhere today, somewhere really public—me, you, and Pete. Let them have their story. As long as you and Ayala believe me that nothing is going on between me and Pete, then I don't feel the need to justify anything to anyone else."

"Believe me—the thought never even crossed our minds." He came around to my chair and pulled me toward him for a deep, wonderful kiss. My lips were on fire where his touched mine, and I felt weak just around the ankles. My body seemed to have a way of responding to him before my brain could, and I pressed into him, totally enraptured by his touch and taste. There was nothing that I wanted more than this, right here, right now.

Sure enough, things settled down in a week or two. Every now and then, I would walk in on an abrupt end to a conversation, but none of this fazed me. I worked hard at my job, and seeing Dunstan practically every day erased any negative energy. Ayala periodically cracked up at Pete's and my "affair," and occasionally, the whole situation made for good dinner conversation at Pete's and my expense.

Dunstan and I dated steadily for a few months, and our romance felt storybook. Whenever Dunstan was in Europe, he would pick me up for lunch, and we spent wonderful afternoons discovering the towns and surrounding villages. Dunstan spent as much time as he could with me whenever he was nearby. We kept our intimate time together out of the public eye, but without sneaking around. We just enjoyed simple things like hikes in the hills and quiet lunches and dinners. We would curl up and watch old movies and occasionally hang out with Pete and Ayala. Although Italy wasn't known for its surfing life, we did venture to Sardinia, where I watched the trio command the waves. I was happy, and nothing was going to change that.

One Sunday, Dunstan invited me for a late breakfast. Despite his pleas to move to his home, I still lived at the cottage on my own, but he had given me a key nonetheless. I was both shocked and pleased at how easily and quickly he had put his complete trust in me. The house was quiet when I arrived; everyone seemed to be enjoying a lazy Sunday. On my way to the kitchen, I passed the music room, and to my delight, Dunstan was there, fiddling with his collection.

"Destiny." He rose, smiling with a grin as bright as the sun. "You are beautiful at every hour of the day." He reached for me and pulled me into a deep, long kiss. "Come, come in and sit with me," he said, nudging me toward the grand piano. "Would you like to try your hand at this?" He motioned for me to sit.

I couldn't help but laugh. "I'm absolutely sure. I wouldn't even know how to open it!"

He furrowed his brow as he studied me intently. "Okay," he said gently, "how about you choose the sounds of the day?" I looked at him curiously, and he continued to explain. "Every now and then, I change out the selections of songs that you hear throughout the house and gardens. Music is my sanity ... keeps me calm."

I moved over his vast collection and ran my fingers across the titles. I paused at the glass case containing the music from his friend and looked back at him quizzically. "Well, I would like to hear more of this artist," I said, pointing to the case.

Dunstan came behind me and took my hand. He opened the case and removed all of the discs. I noticed that "DAT" was written on them. He removed them one by one, almost reverently, and placed them into the complicated-looking piece of equipment hidden creatively behind a wall panel. He set the discs to randomly play, and it wasn't too long before I joined him in his reverie as the haunting, beautiful soundscapes coursed through my mind. He interlaced his fingers with mine, and the touch of his hand sent thrills through me. His grip was firm yet gentle, and my hand grew warm. His thumb absently played across my fingers as we listened together; he seemed to be observing me and eventually pulled me closer to him.

"Have you ever wondered about your parents, your family?" he asked gently.

"At first I did. But after I couldn't find anything on myself, I figured that I was alone even before the accident. I mean, how could there be someone out there if I couldn't find them? There was absolutely no trace of me or my life anywhere. At first that freaked me out a bit, but now I guess I'm okay with it. Maybe one day I might try to trace my history or something once again, but to be honest, I don't have a burning need to know where I came from." I paused and touched the side of his face. "At least not right now."

Dunstan took my hand and kissed it gently. Now that we were on the topic of family, for the first time Dunstan opened up about life with and without his parents. He seemed really at ease and talked at his own pace. He described how after he lost his mother how his father had buried himself in his work; this seemed to be the only thing that could help his father retreat from the pain threatening to overtake him.

"I love the arts and music," Dunstan said with a faraway look in his eyes. "Books are all I really had in my teenage years. My dad and I moved to Europe shortly after my mom died, and he became a little bit of a recluse. I filled my time with books and my father's work. Even though we were far away from everything, I loved living where we did. I guess I missed having a mom, but I didn't really know that life—you know, a life with a mother and father—so I guess I adapted quickly."

I peered out the expansive bay window that overlooked the gardens. The foliage below was now a rustic orange, and wherever the sun's rays touched, everything seemed to glow. I looked slowly around, and finally my eyes rested on Dunstan's face. His eyes held the sun and seemed to become iridescent as he turned his head to me and smiled. He was breathtaking. I couldn't help but feel overwhelmed every time I looked at him.

"Dunstan?" I said. He shifted his gaze to me once again. "I'm sure you get this all the time, but I have never seen anything like you."

He raised his eyebrows quizzically, a wide grin spreading on his face, illuminating his stare even more and making him impossibly more beautiful. "Thing? You called me a thing?" He laughed.

"You know what I mean," I said, embarrassed at my failed attempt to flirt. I swatted him in playful anger. "Don't laugh. I'm serious. It's like you are not of this world or something. You're flawless," I gushed.

He blushed and stroked my hair—the act was beginning to be a favorite of his, and mine. "Well, Desti, I have been called a thing or two in my lifetime—but not alien." He leaned in with a mischievous grin, and I punched his arm.

Dunstan arose and playfully bowed with an outstretched arm. I chuckled and rose to meet him, and soon, the music took over once again. The symphony exploded in my mind like a brilliant pattern across the night sky. After a while, Dunstan broke the silence. "I haven't stopped thinking about you, at all, not since we met, to be honest," he said quietly as he pulled me close.

I could hear the pounding of his heart as I rested my head on his chest. I inhaled the beauty of him and reminded myself that this was all real, that everything beautiful that I had ever known was now overshadowed by the experiences of the last few months. As we swayed to the tunes, soft vocals joined the composition now filling my head. I could remember each line of the tune as soon as I heard it.

Listen to the midnight orchestra of lovers
Senselessly chirping in the night.
Inhale the interrupted stillness of dew
Settling on stalks, waiting for early light.
Place the intrusion of heavy engines in a net
Of quiet, and slowly inhale moist air.
Listen to the unnoticed melody
And capture a salty wind blowing near.
Pay attention to the sights and smells
And greet each thought with revere.
Revel in the beauty of an untouched night
And realize that you are here.

I was overcome with emotion as the tune painted a scene in my head so brilliant and so clear that I was frozen. It was then that Dunstan cupped my chin and lifted my face toward his. With slightly trembling hands, he drew me close and put his lips gently on mine. I was captivated by the taste of him and soon engulfed in a frenzy that started from deep within. I put my arms around his neck and interlaced my fingers as he pulled me into him. I was hot and cold at the same time; I couldn't explain how incredibly safe and wanted I felt in his arms. If someone could have taken a snapshot of what was going through my head, they would have been blinded by the sight.

When we finally parted, he tilted my head toward him and exhaled slowly. "Each time I kiss you, it's like kissing you for the first time. You're breathtaking," he said softly.

"So are you." I knew then that I was falling in love. I paused before continuing, my voice wavering slightly as I spoke. "I feel as though I've known you for a very long time." I ran my fingers across his eyebrow. He closed his eyes and caught his breath. He opened his eyes slowly, looked beyond me for a split second, and then exhaled slowly as he seemed to come to a decision of some sort.

"Come sit with me. There is something that you must know." He walked me over to the couch facing the window and motioned for me to sit.

I held my breath for fear that I had said too much, felt too much too soon. I waited with bated breath, not knowing what was coming next but fearing the worst.

He began slowly, with a faraway look in his eye. "Desti, what I'm about to tell you may sound incredulous, but it's true. I will answer all of your questions as honestly and as directly as I can. There is nothing that you can't ask me." His voice was tender and kind as he looked me in the eyes, but I was already worried.

I hadn't noticed that Pete had entered the room until he sat beside me. He looked quizzically at Dunstan.

"She's ready, Pete. We have to tell her," Dunstan said, as if Pete had asked him a question. Dunstan exhaled and turned back to me. "Destiny, do you believe in soul mates?"

I shrugged my shoulders. "Not until recently," I replied, trying to make light of the pensive mood, a bit embarrassed yet curious as to why Pete was now in the room.

Dunstan continued. "Desti, the last few months have been amazing—for all of us." He looked over at Pete. "We've felt and learned so much, and I know what is happening between us is very real." He looked at me intently. "The reason for this is that you have been a part of my life for a very long time. Everything changed on the day that you fell."

I leaned forward now, my interest fully piqued.

Pete now touched my hand. "You know how we always joked around about sharing the same last name?" he began. I nodded, curious as to where this was all leading.

"Well, Desti, we share the same last name because you are my sister," Pete said. He paused to allow me to digest the news.

I looked at both Dunstan and Pete, sitting seriously around me, and broke out into hearty laughter. "Yeah, right. Okay, you got me. Is *Punk'd* still a show? Where are the cameras?" My smile faded as I noticed that neither of them smiled in return, and no cameras appeared either. "What? Are you serious right now? My brother?" I put my arm next to Pete's and pointed out my dark skin in comparison to Pete's lightly tanned arm. "Impossible! What's going on?" I trembled a little as I stood, but I was still a bit interested in what they had to say.

"Desti, please," Dunstan pleaded. "There is no real right way to break this all down, but we are going to try. All I ask is that you hear us out."

Chapter 13

———~ww∘∘ϵↄ∘ϵↄ∘∘ww———

D unstan took a deep breath. "From what we understand, there are at least two dimensions—this one and ours. Who knows, there may be many more, but these are the two that we know of. In short, we are not from this dimension— and Desti, neither are you." He paused, waiting for my reaction, it seemed. I stared straight ahead, so he continued.

"Jumping is for a select few in our dimension. The possibility is not known to the wider public in our dimension and is definitely unknown here. We are not allowed to bring anyone originating in this dimension over. When we jump, our bodies stay in our dimension in a kind of suspended animation. It's our minds that complete the jump into who we are here."

I was confused. "So now you are saying that there are two of me?" I asked.

"Well, kind of—of each of us," Dunstan said. "We've done quite a bit of research on this. Our dreams and subconscious are more intelligent than we think them to be; they are especially greater than what people here in this dimension think. The two consciousnesses merge in a jump that is completed properly. So when we jump here, we merge our memories, thoughts, and emotions with the person that we are here. Our bodies remain in the first dimension. It's a very controlled process as you can imagine."

"And then we have to rejuvenate," Pete interjected. "We should really only stay for seven or eight days here before returning to rejuvenate."

"Rejuvenate?" I asked.

"Yes. You see, while our consciousness is in this dimension, the body begins to age exponentially in the first, and we have to jump back to go through a process we called rejuvenation," Pete replied. "Seven days here is about fourteen years on the other side. But the good thing is that it takes us only a few hours to turn back the aging process."

I decided to play along, just to see how much more incredulous the story would become. "So what happens to the body from this dimension when you jump back? Does it forget?" I asked.

"It goes to sleep—what you call REM sleep," said Pete. "Sometimes this consciousness experiences situations and circumstances that the other is experiencing. It's a little like having a dream that feels so real even though you know you've never experienced the events in the dream. Sometimes we stay linked, so we can wake and continue on as if the other has jumped."

"Déjà vu is another experience in this dimension that is linked to ours," added Dunstan. "The person experiencing déjà vu actually has lived the experience—just in our dimension. But we haven't quite figured out how that works, especially with people who we know haven't jumped or tried to. This is why we figure there is so much more about this that we don't know. In fact, I don't believe that we have even scratched the surface."

"With your accident and all that has happened since then," said Pete, "new discoveries are made practically every day, or new theories tested. But what is of utmost importance to us is that we maintain a balance, which is why everything is super controlled. We've seen the results of good jumps and bad jumps—on both sides."

"Like what?" I asked.

"Sometimes," Pete continued, "when we don't complete a jump, the body here will awake and be aware of everything but will not be able to get up or move—what is widely known as sleep paralysis. It feels like there is something pressing down on the body. The two consciousnesses are only partially joined, with one being alert and the other still dormant. Eventually, when we are able to pull ourselves back over in our dimension, the person here is able to awake and move."

"It also explains what people here in this dimension call dementia," said Dunstan with a sad look in his eyes. "When a jumper dies in our dimension without properly detaching from this dimension, the person that they are here fades away—like someone with Alzheimer's."

"On the flip side, certain types of schizophrenia are another product of a bad jump when the jumper doesn't properly attach," said Pete.

I'd finally heard enough. "It's as simple as that? All of this world's unexplained brain disorders can be explained by one process—what you call jumping?" My tone was a bit more sarcastic than I'd intended, but it conveyed what I was feeling. "I guess it all makes sense to me now!"

"That we know of. I mean, we still have the same diseases that are products of viral infections, heredity, and cancer. We are still very much alike," Pete replied.

"So what are you saying? There are millions of cases of schizophrenia and Alzheimer's or dementia or whatever—are you saying that the conditions of all of these people are a result of people in your dimension trying to jump?"

"No," Pete answered. "What I am saying is that we have been able to find a definitive link between people who have these diseases and jumpers whose attempts have gone awry. We still don't know enough."

"There was an accident seven years ago, in my dad's lab," said Dunstan, "that helped to pioneer the jumping environment. It was that accident that caused us to lose you. The worst day of my life."

"Okay," I said as I rose calmly.

"Okay?" Dunstan asked, following me as I walked toward the door. "We've just shared the most incredulous story you will probably ever hear, and all you have to say is 'okay'? Please, Desti, you must have questions for us."

"Oh, I have a host of questions, all right." I whirled around to face them both. "I don't know what kind of sick game you two are up to, but you don't do things like this. You don't pull pieces of a person's life and piece together a tale all in the name of a good laugh," I said angrily, almost yelling. "This isn't funny. You aren't funny at all."

"And you," I said, recoiling from Dunstan's attempt to touch me. "How could you do this to me, just when I was falling …?" I couldn't be in the same room with them anymore. I whipped around to run out of the room, forgetting the panel in the wall that Dunstan and I had opened earlier to access his music equipment. I crashed into it full force and put my hand to my forehead, where a trickle of blood soon began.

"Desti!" Dunstan cried, running to my side instantly. He was able to catch me before I slumped to the ground. Pete was there at my side also as the room began fading. In my last moments of consciousness, I was sure that I could hear Pete speaking, except his lips weren't moving. A wave of nausea hit me then, and the room faded away.

Chapter 14

—◦◦◦◦◦◦◦◦◦—

The room was white and quiet, and the sheer linen curtain was blowing in the breeze. One, two, three, four, five, six—the lights flashing in my head coincided with the tolling of the church bells in the distance, signaling the change of the hour. I slowly sat up and rubbed my aching head. Another vision of white appeared, and soon I was able to focus my eyes on Dunstan. I sat up, confused.

"Where am I? What happened?" I asked.

"You took a nasty fall. It's a minor concussion—nothing to worry about," Dunstan answered, moving immediately to my side. He poured a glass of water and offered it to me. "Are you all right?"

"I think so. I mean … I don't know." I thanked him and took a sip of the water. "I feel different somehow," I said.

Once again, Dunstan looked beyond me, and Pete entered the room shortly after. His brow was wrinkled with concern as he looked at me.

"How are you feeling?" Pete came to my side and checked the small bandage that had been applied to my forehead. "You gave us a scare for a little while, Desti. You knocked yourself out cold."

"Where am I?" I asked again, sipping the water tentatively. My head throbbed but not like before. I felt out of sorts somehow and figured it was due to the fall. It was then that the conversation with

Dunstan and Pete came flooding back to me all at once. I raised myself as quickly as I could, again becoming acutely suspicious of the two men in the room with me.

"You are at the infirmary here on the compound at corporate; we brought you down here after your collision, just to be safe," Dunstan replied. There was an awkward moment of silence as we both waited on the other to speak.

I broke the silence. "So," I said tentatively, "what you guys were telling me earlier—you weren't horsing around?"

Pete shook his head and looked at Dunstan, who shook his as well. "We just want you to know the truth and know that you will never be alone now that we have found you," Dunstan said. "We're going to figure out a way to get you through this." His eyes darkened, and he leaned in to fluff my pillow.

Despite the incredulous tale that I had been told, I found that I was still incredibly attracted to him as he drew closer to me, and for a split second, I wanted to forget the last few hours and revel in the encounters we had shared before. I then recalled something else. I turned to Pete.

"Pete, just before I blacked out, I swear that I could hear you, except you weren't speaking. I know it sounds crazy, but I'm certain that I could hear you talking."

It was Pete's turn to become pensive. "That's because you have a special gift, like us." He gestured to Dunstan and to himself. "We have the gift of a kind of telepathy. Since you and I were both adopted, we didn't know if this was an inherited gene. Back home, neither of us remembered when we 'heard' our first thought, and we could only hear people if they too shared the same gift. So in other words, we weren't going crazy from hearing thousands of thoughts at one time. In fact, our lives were quite normal. We always thought it strange that our parents had adopted two kids with the same gift, but we never really questioned it. Our mom had said that we were destined to be a family, and so we accepted that.

"The way that we explain it is that whereas the average person uses their brain at, say, volume two, we have the ability to raise our volumes to four or five. We can either tune in or tune out. You hardly ever used your gift because you found it intrusive and rude. Maybe that's why you aren't able to use it over here now."

I didn't know what to believe anymore. I knew that all of this was crazy, but I couldn't deny what I had experienced, which made me begin to question my disbelief. My head hurt, and suddenly I felt very tired. I leaned back into the pillows and closed my eyes. I needed to think. I needed to be away from this place and this crazy story and, most of all, away from Dunstan, whose presence was intoxicating and hindering me from thinking straight.

"I'm really tired, and I would like some time to rest," I said, opening my eyes and focusing on Pete and Dunstan, who also looked suddenly tired.

"Okay," Dunstan said, though he looked concerned. "The past few hours have been tough on us all. You get some rest and give either of us a call when you are ready to talk some more." He kissed me gently on the forehead before unwillingly retreating. Pete also bade me farewell, and soon I was alone.

I stared out at the beautiful scenery below. I did not know what to think, feel, or believe. Could this incredible story be real? I thought about my inability to remember anything. I couldn't get Dunstan out of my mind—he wouldn't play such a cruel trick on me, would he? Up to this morning, I had been sure of my feelings for him, but with all this—what did this mean? After all these years of being alone, they were my ... family? Why were they only telling me now? If any of this was true, how could they have left me on my own for so many years? I shook my head. What was I thinking? None of this could be true. There must be some sort of explanation, but I wasn't sure that I was willing to find out what it was. Overwhelmed, I suddenly felt the room closing in around me. I called the only person I could think to call: Ethan. I was gone within the hour.

Chapter 15

I was starting a new job in a few days, and I was taking advantage of as much leisure time as possible. My newfound love of music had led me to enroll in a few night classes, and I was surprised at the speed at which I was learning and loving it. My headaches had subsided considerably, but my already strange dreams had now become more intense, vivid, and stranger than I'd ever experienced before, and they left me feeling exhausted and bothered each morning. I had compartmentalized Dunstan, Pete, and Ayala in a box and tucked them away in the back of my mind. I thought over the note I'd left them all, asking them never to contact me again—basically calling them all quacks. It was a bit harsh, but it was what I felt. I knew that I had made the right decision—at least that was what I told myself each time memories of them flooded and clouded my mind.

I looked wistfully at the crashing tide and sipped the last of my drink. I knew that I had made the right decision in leaving. It was all just too much. The more I thought about what had happened back in Italy, the more convinced I was that it had all been part of some cruel practical joke. Ethan and Stella had helped me get set up in a tiny yet affordable apartment on the West Coast back in the USA, and I vividly remembered the smug smirk on Vera's face as I bade farewell to the rest of the team. I had heard nothing from Dunstan since leaving the house in the hills of Italy, nor had I seen or heard from my supposed brother. It was probably better that way—I wanted to disappear.

Yet even after all of this, I longed for Dunstan every day, which I found very frustrating and confusing. I shrugged off these thoughts and sighed. Today, I had decided to go surfing. With no job, I was living on my accumulated savings and was being cautious with spending, but I needed something to do to pass the time. I felt like the ocean had been calling to me, and every day I found myself drawn to the pounding waves and frothy surf. When my surfing instructor was impressed by how quickly I had mastered the waves, I quickly shut down Pete's voice in my head telling me that I had been a good surfer in another life.

I went inside to gather my things, passing the television on the way. I was reaching for the remote to switch it off when, as my luck would have it, Dunstan's face appeared. I knew that it was a bad idea to watch, but it was the first time I had seen him in almost six months, and I couldn't help but sit. I turned the volume up on the news program. He was still as handsome as he'd been on the first day I laid eyes on him, but he also looked tired and sad as he announced that Dream Scape Inc. was closing its doors. The report then flashed to several of the offices as employees reacted to the news of the closure. And there was Pete, quiet and stoic, not speaking to any reporters, with Ayala at his side, as they exited their car and entered the corporate office. I couldn't believe what I was seeing. I remained seated for a long time even after I had switched off the TV. It was none of my business, I eventually told myself, and I grabbed my board and headed through the door.

Strangely enough, when I was out there on my own on the ocean, I didn't feel alone. But today I felt bothered and distracted. After getting pounded a few times, I decided to call it a day. I couldn't shake the gloominess of the faces that I had grown to love in a short space of time. On top of that, there were all the people who would now be without jobs. *Could all this be happening because of me?* I wondered. *Impossible. But … what if?*

I ran back to my apartment. I needed to talk to Dunstan, but the number I'd used to reach him since the day I sprained my ankle was no longer in service, so I called Ethan on his mobile. He answered on the second ring but sounded distracted. "Hi, Desti. Are you okay?" he asked.

I didn't know where to begin. I'd never shared with anyone the real reason I'd left Dream Scape Inc. The story was too incredible to tell. At times I felt like I at least owed Ethan an explanation, but I couldn't bring myself to say anything, and he never pressed me either. I sighed and asked if he was busy.

"I'm just finishing up a few things. What do you need?" he asked.

"I need a huge favor. I really need to get into contact with Dunstan—I mean, Mr. Moab," I said.

Ethan was quiet for a few seconds. "Is everything okay?" he asked.

"I'm fine—really, I am—but I do need to reach him as a matter of urgency," I replied.

Ethan was silent once again. I held my breath, waiting for him to ask the dreaded why question, which I couldn't and didn't want to answer.

Instead, he finally said, "I guess I can help you out with that, if you are sure that this is what you want … Hold on."

Ethan put me on hold, and a few seconds later, a familiar voice answered. "Destiny?"

It was Dunstan. I held my breath now, not sure what to say since I wasn't expecting Ethan to be with him. It felt like the words were caught in my throat, and I had to shake them out.

"Desti," Dunstan said once again, "are you okay?"

"Yes ... yes, I am." I suddenly felt very tired, and a part of me regretted both my rash decision to leave and my decision now to call. But both acts were done, and there was nothing I could do except say what I thought. "Listen, Dunstan, I don't know all the reasons you have decided to close the company, but I just wanted to ask you to think of all the people that have grown to love Dream Scape Inc. I'm just asking you to reconsider."

There was silence on the other end. Finally, I heard Dunstan exhale slowly. "Destiny, you were the only reason for us to be all here. You've made it clear that you want nothing to do with us, with me ... so it's time for us all to go home." I swallowed hard as he continued. "I promised you that I would never cause you any kind of pain, and maybe it was selfish and cruel of me to lay this all on you, and I'm so sorry if I've hurt you in any way. This is the right thing for us to do—to let you move on with your life here without any reminders of a past that you really don't know about. So good-bye." With that, Dunstan was gone. The tears fell from my eyes without my even realizing it.

Dunstan handed the phone back to Ethan and excused himself. He inhaled the crisp air and felt his eyes moisten. He knew that he was doing what was best for her, but he couldn't believe that he was saying good-bye. He had no choice because her note had been crystal clear—she didn't believe anything they had told her, and she wanted to be left alone. The only way that he could ensure her happiness was to give her what she wanted, even though it broke his heart. Pete came in just then.

"We'll be ready to make the final jump at the end of the week," he said quietly. "Are you sure you want to do this? I mean, I know Destiny—she is as stubborn here as she is back home—but once she has had some time to think things through, I believe she will come around."

It was a while before Dunstan answered. "It's been six months. Yes, Pete, we have to leave her alone. Maybe we ... I was being selfish. I never thought through what all of this could do to her. I just wanted to find her, bring her home. I never really thought about how disruptive the process would be, how incredulous our story would seem to her. And now she practically has to start all over again." He looked away reflectively.

Chapter 16

———◦◦◦◦◦◦◦———

D unstan watched Destiny take the waves again. She was oblivious to the fact that he was there, just a few minutes' walk away from the place she had moved to, and he intended to keep it that way. He wanted to see her one last time before he returned to Italy to make his final jump for good. Hearing her voice on the phone had taken him back to wonderful yet painful memories, and as much as he'd wanted to beg her to reconsider, he knew that he couldn't.

He thought back to their first official date as he sat on the balcony and watched her cut through the waves expertly and gracefully. He thought about reaching out to her telepathically, but he didn't want to scare and upset her any more than she already was. Instead he let his mind wander again to the past; maybe, he thought, sitting here on the outside of the rented villa, watching her in the distance while remembering the times they had shared back in his dimension, was a fitting way to say good-bye.

He remembered how the setting sun had caught the gold flecks in her eyes during their evening stroll. He had to smile as he recalled her explanation of her adorable habit of walking backward at times. When he'd asked about it, she had simply said, "Just taking it all in. Sometimes you have to slow down and look back to enjoy what's in front of you even more."

That evening, he had arrived at Destiny's apartment to pick her up to attend a concert in the park, and they had decided to share a cool walk there. Pretty soon, they were lost in conversation and thoughts as they walked along one of the western trails of the school. They were all students at Cal Ed University, a very private school for the gifted; the school focused on students who were academically gifted in either science or the arts, and students' other "gifts" were kept quiet. Dunstan and Destiny both found that weird and spent some time trying to guess which gift some of their classmates had.

They talked about everything that they could think of, and it felt as though they had known each other for a lifetime. Dunstan listened with deep interest when she described her family's life in Hawaii, and Destiny listened with clear empathy when he talked about the passing of his mother and his life in Europe with his dad.

He was wearing faded jeans and a light blue T-shirt, the latter of which apparently caused his eyes to reflect a brilliant blue. He laughed when she told him that all he had to do was look at her through deliciously long lashes, and she was a goner.

She told him how much she missed Hawaii—the freshness of it, the incredible sunsets, the surf, and even the volcanoes. "I miss it a lot sometimes. I could get lost there, you know, really compose my music—it's like everything bad is filtered out, and only light comes in," she said thoughtfully as she recalled endless evenings she had spent watching the sun kiss the world good night. "Living there, you had no choice but to be happy—there was just too much beauty around you. I can't really remember any time that I was really upset or depressed for more than five minutes. I could just take off, you know—really escape. I loved living in Hawaii. Our house, my family life, me, Pete, and Mom and Dad—it was like we lived in our own perfect world.

"I guess I realize now how important the concept of having a family is to me, especially since I almost ended up not having one.

I think that being separated from the people I love probably cuts me deepest. I don't know if I could survive without having at least one member of my family around.

"My dad said that Hawaii reminded him of women—every type of emotion in one place, romantic and exotic at some times, calm and soothing at others, angry and explosive but nurturing at the same time."

Dunstan laughed at this statement and agreed.

"When Pete left for school, I felt as though a piece of me had disappeared. I couldn't explain it. I didn't let my parents know, but there were some days that I couldn't breathe for how much I missed his zaniness," she said thoughtfully. She admitted that she was surprised that she was telling him so much in such a short space of time and with such ease. But he encouraged her to continue, and so she did.

"My parents worked all the time and traveled a lot, so I took my surfing and my music to another level to pass the time. The surfing over there is fabulous. You could really push yourself, you know? You learned a lot about who you were and your strength. A lot of my best pieces, I wrote just sitting watching a sunset after a few good sets. Just when the sun lit up the sky, as it was about to crest, the pattern of my compositions would form."

"I've never been to Hawaii," Dunstan said. "Sounds like someplace I'd like to see some day. Any volunteers for a tour guide?"

"Maybe," Destiny said, snuggling closer to him as they walked along.

"Speaking of music," he continued, "did you ever finish that piece you were working on when we met at the bonfire?"

"It's almost done. I haven't quite gotten the ending yet," she replied.

"Please share. I haven't been able to get the first bit out of my head," Dunstan urged, using his gift with her for the first time in a while.

She thought of the notes that she had finished, and at the end of it, Dunstan experienced some difficulty containing his thoughts. His accolades of praise clearly thrilled her.

"*I decided to call it Gray Skies.*" And then she told him why, shyly touching the outer crease of his gray eyes. He thought it was sweet. At first, she thought that he was being kind, but then she saw that he was genuinely pleased that she'd named her piece after him.

Soon, they were sitting in an alcove with a few other students. It was then that the blonde from the bonfire passed by. She greeted Dunstan, totally ignoring Destiny, leaving her date unattended. When Dunstan draped his arm around Destiny, she waved goodbye, but took a position in the shaded benches just across from where they were seated.

"Hey, I hope I'm not spoiling your rep here," Destiny said jokingly, jabbing him in the ribs.

He chuckled. "That's Vera. She never quits—I'll give her that." He pulled her closer and said, "Desti, there is no one else I'd rather be with right now, right here, than you." He gently tucked her hair behind her ear, and his fingers lingered on the side of her face for a few seconds.

"*You're so beautiful, Desti. You are mesmerizing,*" he said, his thoughts feeling more personal than spoken words.

"*Thanks, Dunstan. You are pretty hot too,*" she replied.

He laughed out loud.

Dunstan sighed deeply and stood, peering out to the ocean one last time. Memories of his teenage romance took him to a place that he knew would lead him to reverse the decision that he had made. He also was worried about the effects on her body in the second dimension. They were able to stay here for only a short period of time, and they aged significantly. Destiny had been here for years. What would be the outcome if she ever decided to jump?

He couldn't risk it. He had decided that if she wanted him, he would stay here and jump whenever necessary to rejuvenate. But now that wasn't an option anymore. He wouldn't and couldn't risk anything happening to her.

He was never going to cause her any more pain. He had promised her that. Besides, he couldn't live in this world knowing that she was right at his fingertips and yet so far away. He watched the bobbing head in the crashing surf and closed the door. He would let her be. She would start over, without him, and she would find and settle her life. He watched Destiny take another wave, and in his heart he bade her farewell for the last time.

Chapter 17

It was just before seven in the morning a few days after my phone call with Dunstan when I heard a light tap on the door. I was already up but had remained in bed, replaying my last conversation with Dunstan. I had been in some sort of daze since then, and I found myself questioning whether I had made the right decision by not trying to hear out his crazy story. The one thing that stuck with me, which I had tried to block out in the previous months, was the experience of hearing voices in my head. I couldn't deny that I had heard both Dunstan and Pete speak to me without saying a word out loud, and this was the one thing that I couldn't rationalize. And what of my new ability to play music and my command of the waves? How could I explain that? What if—just what if all they had said was true? I startled when I heard the light tap again. I crawled out of bed, trudged to the bathroom and splashed some water on my face. I peeked through the window, and to my surprise, there was Stella. I opened the door and invited her in.

"I'm so sorry to bother you at this time in the morning," Stella said, "but I've really got to talk to you."

"Okay," I replied. "Please come in and have a seat. Would you like a cup of coffee?" Stella nodded, and I moved to get a pot brewing. I then excused myself to brush my teeth. On my return,

Stella was pacing the tiny living area. She had opened the windows, letting in the chilly ocean air.

"Stella," I said, "why are you here? Does Ethan know you are here?"

"No, Ethan left for Italy late last night—finalizing the closing. I had to come to see you, Destiny. There are things that you should know," Stella replied.

I noticed that Stella was trembling a bit as she took the mug of coffee that I offered. "Please sit down. What's going on?"

"I don't know where to start—how to start," Stella said, taking a sip of the fresh brew. She exhaled deeply and toyed nervously with the mug. "Great coffee, by the way … Destiny, what I'm about to say to you will sound absurd, and I am sure you will have some difficulty believing any of it. All I'm asking is that you hear me out—beginning to end." Stella raised her eyes to look at me, and for the first time, despite her ageless beauty, Stella's eyes seemed tired.

I couldn't help but roll my eyes, recalling another tale that had started exactly like this one. Stella set her coffee down forcefully enough that some spilled over the rim. "Promise me," Stella said. I nodded, filled with curiosity despite my wariness.

"I know Pete and Dunstan started to tell you about their lives, their past. I can only imagine what a difficult pill that was to swallow, and I fully understand why you decided to leave. I just wanted to share my story with you, to see if it could help change your mind and maybe convince you to help Dunstan."

"I don't understand, Stella … I mean, why are you here?" I asked, now more curious than ever.

"There really is no good or easy way to tell you about this," Stella said quietly. She exhaled deeply before continuing. "You see, there is something you have to know about the Moab men—when they love, they love hard. There is nothing else like it." She paused, and her eyes seemed to glaze over, as if she was recalling another lifetime.

"You see, what feels like a lifetime ago, I found out that I was dying. I was suffering from a very rare disorder similar to an adult form of progeria. When we found out what my future was, the ultimate sacrifice was made. Rather than see me waste away to nothing, Dunstan's dad found a way to jump me here."

I choked slightly on my coffee. I was about to interject, but Stella raised her hand, stopping me. "You see, I am Dunstan's mother." Tears brimmed in Stella's eyes almost instantly, but she continued. "We told Dunstan that I was sick when he was very young, and after I jumped, his father told him I had died. We decided to let me remain dead to him so that he could have a life without ever trying to find me. You see how he is with you—he has never given up in his search for you. His dad is just like that, and he knew that Dunstan's life would be spent trying to find or cure me if he knew. Ironically, as fate would have it, here we all are."

"So you are saying that you are from their world?" I asked, my tone part patronizing and part disbelieving.

"*Our* world," Stella said gently. "You promised to hear me out."

I raised both hands in acquiescence, and Stella went on.

"You see, I was the first jumper. Dunstan's dad—he figured out a way to get me into this dimension, and here my disease had a reverse effect on my body. At least this is what we think has slowed my aging. I'm aging here, but a bit slower than normal." She wrung her hands nervously as she continued. "I made the hardest decision I've ever had to make. I saw the pain my husband went through, seeing me suffer every day, and I wasn't going to let that happen to Dunstan." Tears welled in her eyes.

"I lived every day in the hope that someday they would figure out a way to come here so that I could see them again. And then I thought of how selfish I was being, because if Dunstan found me, then he would be torn; he would have to choose which parent to be with. So I gave him up—for a better life in his world, where he belonged. I asked his dad never to jump to see me again, so that he could move on with his life and focus on raising Dunstan the best that he could."

By now, she was openly crying, and she hid her face in her hands. "I wanted him to move on with his life, and I wasn't going to let my only son grow up without either parent. His dad was risking his life enough as it was, and I loved them both too much, enough to let them go," Stella said.

My jaw dropped. "So you knew about me all along, and you didn't tell me?" I was now trembling with rage. "Ethan—all this time, he knew what was going on too, and he let me suffer? All alone, scared, confused. And Dunstan ... all Ethan's talk about looking out for me, warning me to stay away from him—he was trying to protect you, not me!" I almost shouted.

"Destiny, it's not like that at all. You are like a daughter to him—to us. We would never do anything to hurt you." Stella was still crying. "We just weren't sure if you were this dimension's Destiny or the other. And besides, would you have believed us?"

I knew that Stella was right. I had to calm down. I hadn't given Dunstan a chance when he'd tried to explain, and I knew that I would have rejected Stella and Ethan's story as well. I went to the window and mulled over everything that I had just heard. I was trying to get hold of the situation in my mind. "So how does Ethan fit into this whole thing?" I asked.

"I met Ethan a few years after I jumped, and he became my confidant. At first I didn't tell him who I was or where I came from, not until you arrived in our lives. You may not believe it, but I cried every night for Dunstan. When I first heard about Dream Scape, I had no clue who Dunstan was until I laid eyes on him. I was clueless as to the advances which had been made on the jump machine, but somehow I just knew that we were connected. I didn't know about the work being done on the other side, and I hadn't seen Dunstan since he was a small boy. But a mother just knows. That was the first and only time that Dunstan's dad broke his promise. He jumped to explain what he thought had happened to you and to ask me to take care of you until they figured out how to get you home. He was there on the day that you fell, and we've been looking out for you ever since then. He also told me that he had told Dunstan about me after the death of your parents and that Dunstan wanted to meet me.

"That night was the hardest night of my life. I had to tell Ethan my history. Like you, he didn't believe me at first, but when I told him that I had a son and who that son was, that was the icing on the cake. I didn't see him for days. Once again, Dunstan's dad came to the rescue. I don't know how he found Ethan or what he said, but by the end of the week, Ethan was home and accepted everything that I told him."

"What happened when you and Dunstan met in this dimension?" I asked, intrigued by the twists and turns of Stella's tale.

"When I saw him for the first time in person, I knew that he was my son. I thought that he would be angry at me, but he was the exact opposite. He was forgiving and gracious and kind. He was the most amazing person that I had met in this lifetime or the other."

I remained quiet and waited for her to continue.

"Dunstan told me of your lives back in his dimension, and it was plain how much he loved you. He lit up when he spoke about you, but I could see the sadness in his eyes. He told me that he would never give up on finding a way to get you back home. He has been waiting all these years for the chance to be with you and present you with a choice."

Stella rose and joined me at the window. She laid her hand on my shoulder and continued. "I came here to you today because of

Dunstan. I know why he is closing Dream Scape. He is giving you want you want. He is leaving for good. I know the sacrifices that the Moab men are willing to make for the women they love. And he loves you—deeply and fiercely. He will never be happy without you, and I am sure that by now you recognize that you will never be happy without him."

A tear slowly trickled down my cheek. "I want to believe you; I really do. I want to believe all this, but I just can't."

Stella turned me around. "Destiny, you must see that this is all true. Something happened to you that made you lose your memory of who you are and where you are really from, but think back over the last seven years of your life. What other truth could there be? And what do you have to lose? Please don't let him lose the opportunity to be happy. His happiness is with you. Don't let another wonderful man go through this world alone, Destiny. Don't miss this opportunity to be with the one that you were made for. You have the rare opportunity to truly be happy."

I knew that Stella was right. I had felt more a part of something in the few months with Dunstan than I had felt in all the life that I could remember. This all had to be real; otherwise, I wouldn't feel so deeply connected—not just to Dunstan, but to Pete and Ayala too. And what about my newfound gifts that I had been trying so hard to ignore? I didn't have any answers, but I did know one thing resolutely: something had linked me and Dunstan, and my fears and uncertainty weren't strong enough to break that link.

Finally, I sighed and asked, "What do I do?"

Chapter 18

⸺◦◦◦⸺

The following night, Destiny was back on the winding road leading to Dunstan's house. The first person Stella had called once Destiny had made her decision was Ethan. He had arranged to get them both back to Italy by private jet, just hours after Dunstan's own arrival in Italy.

Ayala greeted her at the door and immediately hugged her fiercely. "Oh, Destiny, I'm so glad that you came back," she said, hugging her even more tightly. "Come, Dunstan is in the pool and doesn't know you're here." Ayala led her through the massive house and up to the top floor, where Dunstan was just emerging and toweling off. He stopped short when he saw them and rubbed the water from his eyes, as if he couldn't believe that Destiny was standing in front of him. Ayala disappeared back inside, leaving them alone.

"Destiny!" he said. In just seconds, without having to say another word, Dunstan and Destiny had covered the distance between them, and Destiny was in his arms. He held on to her, overjoyed but clearly confused too. He gently withdrew from her enough to look into her eyes. "I don't understand. What are you doing here?"

Destiny gently pushed a wet tendril from his forehead. "Believe me, I've been asking myself that question since the minute I stepped foot on the plane," she replied. "But I shouldn't have just left the way that I did. This is all overwhelming, but I can't let you leave or disappear just like that." She pulled away from him and walked over to the edge of the pool, her emotions in turmoil. Being here with him at this very moment was stirring something within her that she couldn't explain, and it frightened her. She had planned everything that she wanted to say, but now everything sounded trivial, and nothing would come out.

"Destiny." She whirled around upon hearing his voice in her head, and Dunstan nodded. *"So you can still hear me."* Dunstan came to her side and looked out to the valley below. *"This must all be very confusing for you, and I get why you don't believe us, but you can't deny the fact that you can hear me—that must count for something."*

Dunstan took her hand tentatively and placed it on his chest. *"Believe me when I say to you, I would never do anything to hurt you. I accept whatever decision you come to, but I felt that you had a right to know that you are bigger than all of this, that you have people who care deeply about you, who want the best for you—who love you.* His beautiful eyes darkened as he said the last words.

Destiny's heart was racing. Stella had told her how much Dunstan loved her, but hearing it from him, especially in such an intimate way in her own mind, overwhelmed her. The tears that had been threatening to spill over since the day she'd run away now overtook her, and she could do nothing else but sob openly. Dunstan took her into his arms and comforted her, embracing her disbelief and fear. Eventually her tears subsided and she raised her head to look at him. Dunstan wiped the tears from her eyes and marveled at how beautiful she still was, through all of this.

"How does this work?" she silently asked. He chuckled, pulled her back to him, and kissed her, almost crushing her with his overwhelming happiness that she was there and beginning to

embrace who she was by using her gifts. And when she wrapped her arms around him and returned his deep embrace, he knew that everything was going to work out and that they would finally be together. The heat between them intensified, and the thirst they felt for each other was such that they were out of breath when they parted. Dunstan couldn't and wouldn't let her go, and even when they sank to the couch overlooking the beautiful scenery below, his lips never parted from hers for more than a few seconds. They laughed and cried at the same time, and Destiny knew that she belonged with him, no matter what crazy circumstances had ripped them apart in the first place. Eventually, she lay quietly on his chest, listening to his thumping heart slow down as he seemed to exhale the weight of the world. Dunstan stroked her hair and her arm and lovingly kissed her head, unable to believe his good fortune. Sometimes he would look down just to make sure that she was there and real.

"*Pete is going to freak out when Ayala tells him,*" Dunstan said.

Destiny caught her breath at the mention of Pete's name. She had a brother. She wasn't alone anymore, and she wanted to find him almost immediately. "Can I see Pete?" she asked.

"Of course you can. He is rejuvenating now—should be out in a couple of hours."

"Rejuvenating?" Destiny asked. "Oh, in other words, he's asleep."

"Yes, more or less," Dunstan said, laughing. They remained silent for a while, each thinking about the next steps.

"*Desti,*" Dunstan finally said, "*I still can't believe that you are here. What changed your mind?*"

Destiny answered tentatively at first, unsure whether she was using her gift right. "*Well … Stella helped me to see what a fool I was for leaving you the way I did.*"

"My mom did this?" Dunstan asked. He laughed out loud. "Our lives are complicated, to say the least. She and Ethan have been looking after you for a very long time from a distance. They are the most amazing set of human beings I know. We are all intertwined somehow, and it appears as though destiny has a design for us all—no pun intended.

"My mom is still so much in love with my dad but can't be with him, and I know that in her own way, she loves Ethan, but it can never extinguish what she feels for my dad. Her disease will never let her return to our time and space, and my dad can't exist here and has accepted that she has another life to live. Ethan is caught in the middle, knowing that the woman he loves will never love him the way that he does."

Destiny inhaled Dunstan's sweet scent mingled with the chlorine from the pool. She couldn't help herself. She was listening attentively to him, but she was still tingling all over from their reunion and intimacy. She had to literally shake herself to snap out of her trance-like fascination with him.

"I don't know if that is the saddest thing I've heard or if our situation trumps them all," she said, gesturing to him and to herself. Even though she smiled, she realized that they were indeed in a tough spot, and the thought sobered her almost instantly.

"The difference is that we now have the technology back home to figure out what happened to you, and second, I will never give up on you or on us, unless you ask me to," he said.

Destiny was silent for a moment, gazing beyond Dunstan, her brow furrowed in thought. "Dunstan, how can we be together? I mean, what is your plan?"

"Well, that is entirely up to you. If you choose to remain here, I can keep jumping and rejuvenating to be with you. We can live here as we are doing now," Dunstan replied.

"But the jumping—that must be taking a toll on your body. I can't ask you to take that risk," she said, holding on to him even tighter.

"There is another option," Dunstan said quietly.

Destiny raised her head. "What? Please tell me."

"Well, we haven't been able to find you here in this world. That is, whereas we all have jumped into our consciousness here, and our bodies remain back home, we have never found who you are here."

"So … I don't understand. Before you jumped, you were exactly who you are now?" Destiny asked, still trying to wrap her head around everything that she was being told.

"Yes," Dunstan replied. "You see, we exist as who we are and who we were. I know it's hard to understand. The best way I can explain it is using an example of sugar and water."

Destiny furrowed her eyebrows and cocked her head to one side, drawing a smile from Dunstan.

"You are so adorable when you do that," he said. He reached for her and kissed her again. Before the passion between the two of them threatened to overpower them again, he withdrew and continued. "If you add sugar to water, you combine the two, and they change. The sugar is still sugar, but the crystals dissolve in the water. The water is still water, but it becomes sweeter because of the sugar. Both the sugar and the water still exist, but they change once mixed. That's what happens when we jump. We are still the same person, but we change once our consciousnesses merge. We become one of both dimensions."

Destiny remained quiet, pondering Dustan's analogy, and then asked, "So what happened to me?"

"Our entire team has only been able to assume that you are here because somehow you jumped altogether like my mom did." He sighed before continuing. "We could try to jump you back altogether."

Destiny thought about what Dunstan was saying. "Dunstan, how did I get here? I mean, what happened?"

"It was after your parents' passing. Nothing could be done to console you. You would speak to no one. When you found out that your parents had actually been working for my dad's company, and it was their work that had taken them in the end, you shut us all out. You shut me out. I tried futilely to reach out to you to explain that I didn't know that your parents were working for Moab Industries, but you refused to see me. You shut every door Pete used to talk to you and wrapped yourself in an impenetrable shell, away from everyone and everything familiar. You didn't write your music anymore; you quit surfing; in fact, you hardly existed.

"A year had almost passed, and I guess Pete was seeking out every intervention tactic he could think of to help you climb out of the dark hole that you had buried yourself in. He suggested—or more accurately, forced—a visit to the lab where your parents spent their last days. He tried to force you to yell, scream, something to get an emotion or reaction out of you. But you would have none of it.

"That was also the time that I found out about my mom, that she was still alive somewhere. I felt lost, rejected by everyone who supposedly loved me. My dad and I, we were barely on speaking terms. Funny enough, Pete was the one who pulled me through that rough time between me and my dad. Pete said he wanted to learn about your parents' work—carry on their legacy. When you found out, you went ballistic. You came to my father's lab, so angry that Pete would be interested in work that might kill him as well."

Dunstan smiled at this point. "Security thought that you were a crazy person and escorted you out of the building." He kissed her forehead, and just then, Charm, her rescued kitten, bounded into her lap. "In fact, it was on that day that you *really* rescued this little mongrel." Dunstan stroked Charm's head, and he began purring instantly. Boxie rounded the corner almost instantly, as if there was a chase on and Charm had gotten the better of him. Dunstan and Destiny both laughed as Boxie whined in complaint and placed his head in Dunstan's lap.

"So Charm is from our world?" Destiny asked slowly. "I tell you – this whole thing gets more and more incredulous."

Dunstan nodded. "He is your cat—seems like you two are destined to be together." He paused at his word association and continued. "At first we didn't know whether or not we could jump animals because we needed a consciousness to assimilate to. But over the past few years, we found that we could actually jump an entire body from one dimension to the next. We did in-depth research on the outcome of my mom's jump, and then chose a cat because of its aging characteristics. In the case of Charm here, he reverted to a kitten—so it took years off of him. When we jumped him back, he went back to his old self.

"The way Charm ages more slowly here than what's normal for a cat seems similar to how my mother's disease, which aged her in our time, slowed down her aging here." Dunstan went quiet then, and Destiny sensed that there was more he wasn't telling her.

"Dunstan, you've got to tell me everything—no more secrets between us if we are going to figure this out." She paused before continuing. "I've decided that I want to be with you, so we have to do this together."

Dunstan couldn't help himself upon hearing Destiny say that she wanted to be with him. He wanted every bit of her mind and body, and he told her so.

He crushed his lips against hers fiercely. They parted but for a brief second, his eyes searching hers. He pulled her on top of him, and their kiss intensified. He had an almost-viselike grip around her as he explored her mind, and a soft moan escaped Destiny's lips as her body cried out for him. Her brain was clouded by an insane sweet pain raging through her body, from lips to toes.

Dunstan held her tighter, his fingers tangling in her hair. His skin was on fire, matching the intense heat spreading inside him. He knew that she loved him and wanted him with everything in her.

His body felt taut and sweet beneath her, and there was nothing she wanted more than this, right now. She pressed into him and kissed his neck and eyelids. She gingerly ran her fingers beneath his shirt as he continued kissing her slowly and sweetly. With eyes closed, she could feel his racing heart against her fingertips, exciting her even more. She thrust her hips against his. His breathing became labored, and he moaned more, as if willing himself to pull away. He was out of breath and almost dizzy from desire when he eventually released her.

"Destiny," he said, inhaling and exhaling slowly, "I know that we have a lot of making up to do, and I don't want to rush into things, but by now you must know that my existence is based on your happiness. There is nothing that can change how I feel about you. I live for your smiles, I yearn for your touch, and I will never stop trying to find a way for us to be together." Dunstan's eyes became bright, sparkling in the light.

"I want you to know that I love you. Destiny, I am so in love with you; every fiber of my being feels like it has been made for you. All of me wants all of you. Forever."

Chapter 19

—⁓⁓◦◦⦾⊶⊷⦾◦◦⁓⁓—

Destiny swallowed on hearing Dunstan's words. She took a deep breath and steadied herself. "I love you too. I knew it from the first night we had dinner in your cabin, but I thought it impossible." Suddenly, she felt a sharp knock in her mind. She couldn't explain it. It wasn't painful, just strange.

"What's wrong?" Dunstan asked, seeing the sudden look of surprise on her face.

"I don't know. I can't describe it—it's like I can hear someone knocking, but up here," she said, pointing to her forehead.

Dunstan smiled. "That's Pete. You told me shortly after we met that you two had a way to knock on each other's doors to talk. I don't know how you do it, but it's something that you practiced as kids growing up. Try focusing on what you felt and see if you can replicate it in your mind."

Destiny closed her eyes and zoomed in on the door that she had seen in her mind's eye. She pictured herself turning its knob, and her eyes snapped open shortly after, when she heard Pete's voice.

"Destiny, I can't believe that you are here!" Pete said.

"Me either, but I'm sure glad that I am. I'm with Dunstan. Can I see you?" she replied.

"Of course—whenever, wherever. I can be there in a minute," Pete offered.

Destiny asked Dunstan if it was okay for her to meet with Pete, and Dunstan offered to give them some time alone. There was so much more that she wanted to learn, but she also wanted to speak with Pete, her brother—her brother. She almost couldn't believe this was real, but on the inside, she glowed at the thought of having a sibling, especially one as beautiful, loving, and fun as Pete.

Pete was true to his word. In just about a minute, his blond head popped around the corner, and he practically ran to Destiny, scooping her up into his arms in a bear hug.

"We used to share loads of these with Dad when we were kids," Pete said, twirling her around and then setting her gently down. "It was a Tallum thing," he added.

They flopped into the couch that she and Dunstan had shared only moments before. "Pete," Destiny said cautiously, "tell me about them, our parents."

Pete smiled and triggered a memory, in Destiny's own mind, of Destiny and their dad shadowboxing before breakfast. He then explained that he had the ability to capture memories shared with him and then recall and transmit the emotions that they evoked.

He watched as Destiny's face lit up until she was almost glowing. "Your memories are there, I think—just closed. We'll get through this," Pete said. "You know how you watch these television families that seem so perfectly happy that you know they aren't real?"

Destiny nodded, still enthralled by what Pete had just shared with her.

"Well, we had that life, and it wasn't fake—we really were that happy." Pete smiled and stretched his long legs. "We loved them both and they loved us, but I think you had a special place in your heart for our dad, and he adored you. Me, I was a mama's boy and proud of it." He laughed. "We did everything together—we hiked, we fished, we played girlie basketball, we surfed, we even went shopping together, even if the latter was painful for me and dad." He laughed again.

"Our dad, he was our hero—we used to draw pictures of him with a cape on as kids, and he loved it. He would hang our so-called art all over the house and make copies of it to take to work. Mom said that it was literally love at first sight when she first laid eyes on him. She often said that it was his 'sea blue eyes' that attracted her, and the rest of him was a bonus. She was a microbiologist, and dad was a physicist. They met working in the R&D of a large cosmetic firm. Five years later, they created and patented a breakthrough regeneration line that made them both very wealthy. They both traveled considerably, although our mom spent the most time away since she was the face of the company.

"You were adopted at the age of one by the husband-and-wife couple of Jenna and Emmanuel Tallum. Mom was the color of smooth chocolate cappuccino, and Dad resembled the foam floating on the top. Together he said that they were the perfect blend. He was corny like that.

"When you were a little girl, you never missed a chance to watch Mom brush her hair or apply her makeup. You would mimic her walk, her laugh, and her facial expressions. She could have been a print or fashion model if she'd wanted. She was beautiful, exotic, and graceful. She was tall and slender with dark inquisitive eyes. She was strong and tough when she needed to be, except when it came to Dad. Then she would melt away with just a wink of his eye.

"Although we never knew our birth parents, I don't think that we missed out on anything. It didn't matter that we weren't conceived by our mom and dad; it always felt like we were conceived *for* them, if you get what I am saying."

Destiny nodded, teary-eyed at the thoughts and memories that Pete was triggering for her as he spoke.

"I was two years old when you joined our family. I was also adopted. You had these big doe eyes that crinkled when you laughed, and Dad would light up whenever you called his name." Pete triggered for Destiny a memory of their dad creeping into her nursery when she was napping and then cooing her to sleep in his own language that she seemed able to understand.

"You were so smart and curious even as a baby, and growing up, I actually didn't mind having you tag along with me; you seemed to fit in every situation, no matter what came up. Plus, you were a ladies' magnet. There was an unspoken girl code for guys who didn't mind their little sisters hang with them sometimes."

"No wonder you all weren't fazed when that business happened with the paparazzi!" Destiny said, suddenly thinking back to the ridiculous stories about her and Pete as well as her and Dunstan. "How silly that all must have been to you, knowing that all along I was your sister!"

Destiny laughed as Peter went on to tell her how he and Ayala had met on the very same day that she'd almost drowned Dunstan. "She took my breath away," he said. "She still does. Every day that I'm with her feels like an adventure. She gets me, and she is forever positive and intelligent. I can't imagine a day without her."

"Does she have our gift?" Destiny asked, tapping the side of her face.

"No," he answered, "but she totally knows about ours. She guessed it, and I couldn't lie to her."

Pete went on to describe life at Cal Ed U, where he had received a full scholarship at the age of fourteen in their advanced medical program, with Destiny joining a few years later. He described their lives at home in Hawaii and how they would sneak out to night-surf whenever there was a full moon. Their dad had often toasted at the dinner table, saying that they had the perfect life, and it was—at least they were all perfect for one another. Occasionally,

Pete brought up specific memories, which he was finding easier and easier to transfer to Destiny, to her delight.

"Pete, what was it like when they died?" Destiny asked.

Pete grew quiet and reflective. "We all took it really hard, Desti. I remember one day you yelled at the waves for almost an hour. The next day, you demanded to be taken to their offices. It was the first time that you had gone near Dunstan in almost a year. After ranting on them until you shook … that's when it happened."

"What happened?" Destiny asked.

"The accident that locked you here. Dunstan and I must've watched the surveillance recording a million times in the last seven years. You slammed your fist on the panel, unknowingly powering up the machine. Then we saw the reactors going crazy. Smoke filled the lab, and then when it cleared, you were gone. We had no clue what had happened to you until Dunstan's dad suggested that maybe somehow you had jumped."

"That's when Dunstan found out about his mom. He told me earlier," Destiny said. A part of her still wished that she could remember everything.

"First, the split between him and you, then finding out that his mom was alive after all these years, and finally, your disappearance— it was enough to send any normal person off the deep end. But not Dunstan—he is like no one else I've met," Pete said.

Destiny thought about how alone Dunstan must have felt in those times, how determined he had to have been in his search for her. Even now, when she had pushed him away for the second time, he had taken it all in stride. Something inside her clicked, and she realized how deeply she was in love with him. She felt intensely attracted to his strength and the beauty of his determination. She had to reel herself back to focus on Pete's words.

"As crazy as it sounded, there was no other explanation," said Pete. "And that is how our search began. We've been searching for a way to bring you home since then. As time passed, we figured out how to jump small animals. Your buddy Charm there is our latest project, except he isn't a kitten back in our time; there he is full grown and still as greedy."

Destiny stroked the kitten's fur, and he lovingly looked up at her, purring happily, as if he knew too that she was back for good.

"There is something else that you should know," Pete continued soberly. "Destiny, we've never successfully jumped anyone physically from this dimension over to ours—for obvious reasons, what we do is completely controlled. We haven't tried it on anyone here, and I don't think that we can. We just don't know what will happen to your body on the other side."

Destiny remained silent for a moment as she contemplated the situation. From the moment that she was in Dunstan's arms once again, she had known that she wanted to return with them, but she had to concede that they might not find a way to get her back safely. She then toyed with the idea of staying here in this world, with Dunstan popping in and out, but she didn't know what effects the jumps might be having on his body and didn't want to put him through any more risk. She had also considered just walking away from it all, given that sometimes when she ran everything through her head, the entire idea seemed ludicrous. She knew, however, that she could not be separated from Dunstan and soon scratched this option off her mental list. She was driving herself zany with all of the questions and fears she had about the future.

"I don't care," she finally said. "I want to be with my family. I want to go home."

Chapter 20

———∿∿◦◦⧸◦⧹◦◦⧸◦⧹◦◦∿∿———

Destiny and Pete must have talked for hours as he filled her in on her life with their parents and Ayala. He talked about her music, their lives at school, and their lives in Hawaii and California. He painted wonderful scenes in her mind when he could, to make those memories feel even more real and convincing. Even though he skimmed over any too-personal or intimate details about her and Dunstan, he did take the time to tell her about the wonderful summer they'd spent with Dunstan when they first met his dad.

"You had no clue who Dunstan really was. It wasn't until we shuttled off in a private jet that it dawned on you that you were enjoying a budding romance with the son of one of the richest and most influential men in the world. I think that was what drew Dunstan to you. You had no clue who he really was, and you wanted to be with him anyway."

"I don't think that it would have made one bit of a difference—have you looked at him lately?" she asked. Pete rolled his eyes in laughter.

Pete went on to describe the gardens of Dunstan's childhood castle home. As spectacular as Dunstan's gardens were in Italy, they apparently paled in comparison to those at his childhood home. Pete described fountains, urns, stairways, guarding lions, marble paths, and other decorative pieces. The interior of the castle was even more of a wonder than the luxurious gardens because of the beauty and richness of the sculpted wood and the stained-glass windows. There was a library as well as a number of legendary paintings, many of which were thought lost; the artworks adorned the hallways to each of the 160 rooms that the group explored during their days there.

"But it was the music room that became your spot," said Pete. "The furniture in the music room was carved of teak, and handmade silk embroideries adorned the ceiling and walls, giving the room a feel of a Turkish salon. Dunstan told us that the ceiling paintings and decorative frescoes had been designed by the renowned Austrian artists Gustav Klimt and Frantz Matsch. His life—it seemed ethereal."

They had all bunked in the tower with its panoramic views of the valley below. Pete shared the memory of Destiny and Ayala squealing as they explored room after room, plus memories of chatting in front of warm nighttime fires, horseback riding on the property's expansive acreage, and scooter biking around on country roads. It was the last happy summer they had shared as a group because by the end of the year, their dad was gone.

"Dad died of accelerated aging. He was a jumper, but the rejuvenation chamber was incomplete, so he couldn't regenerate his cells. And Mom … well, when he died, the grief was just too much. She poured herself into her work, trying to finish what they'd been working on." This was the first time that Destiny had seen no trace of a grin on Pete's face; he was solemn as he spoke of their parents.

"He had told her that he'd found himself in this dimension and that they were together here. She tried to perfect the machine so that she could jump here to be with him. But the chamber still wasn't perfect, and soon she too succumbed to the aging process."

Destiny thought about all this for a while. She remembered how alone and lost she'd felt when she was discovered with no memory. She never wanted to experience that again. Now she had a family, and as crazy as all of this sounded, it felt right to her. She yawned and realized that she had gone almost a day and a half without sleep.

Pete walked with her back into the house and paused outside of Dunstan's door. "We've been talking for hours, so I'm sure he's rejuvenating, but I am all sure that yours will be the first face that he wants to see when he wakes."

Destiny smiled and kissed her brother on the cheek before burying her head in his chest. She felt safe and secure knowing that she was no longer alone. Pete pulled her braid, and something seemed to happen in her brain—this simple act felt familiar somehow. She shrugged it off and bade him good night.

Dunstan's room was dark and cozy, and Destiny could hear his gentle breaths as he slept. She crawled in next to him, and in the faint light provided by the clock on the side table, she studied his face; she had to admit that he was almost too perfect to be from here. She was tired but too excited to fall asleep. She laid her head on his chest, and as she listened to the rhythm of his heart, something started to happen. The beats began to transform into colors and iridescent shades of light. In her mind she heard the sounds of timbrels and brass, and piece by piece, a composition started to form in her head. She had never experienced anything like this before, at least not that she could remember, and she gave herself to the process evolving within her.

Within an hour, she was nodding off to sleep, a full composition penned on a notepad which she found on Dunstan's nightstand.

Soft purring awoke her the next morning as Charm nuzzled her. The sun was barely climbing over the horizon when she stirred. Her head rested comfortably in the crook of Dunstan's arm as he slept with parted lips. She couldn't describe what she was going through, and as she drew doodles with her eyes on the ceiling, she sighed. The gentle rhythm of Dunstan's breathing lulled and relaxed her. She toyed with Charm's tail as he began purring in tune with Dunstan's breathing. She didn't have the urge to change positions, but soon Dunstan stirred.

"Good morning," he said into her hair. He kissed her on the forehead. "I could get used to this." They lay quietly for a few minutes, both reveling in the events of the day before.

Destiny chose her words carefully. "Dunstan, we might not see it now, but we have all been reunited at this time, at this point, for a reason. I would do anything to have never been separated from you in the first place, but it happened; there is nothing we can do to change any of this. But I am never going to let anything come between me and anyone I love ever again."

She interlaced her fingers even tighter with Dunstan's, and it was a while before he responded. He exhaled slowly and turned to face Destiny.

"I guess you are right, Desti. I hope that by now you know how much I love you—how much I want to be with you. I will do anything to be with you—for the rest of my life. But I can't endanger you in any way or put you at risk. For the first time in a very long time, I just don't know what my next move should be."

"Dunstan, we are going to figure this out together. If I have to remain here, I will, in the knowledge that I have you in some form. And if you have to stop jumping because of whatever ill effects that the jumps are having on your body, then I will accept that too, and I will always have you in my heart."

"I don't even want to think about that. I can't even conceive it," Dunstan said with resolve in his voice. They lay in silence before Destiny continued.

"Dunstan, I want to be with you. Can we have double lives? Can we both coexist as we are now, until we figure things out?

I mean, why we are in a rush for a solution? I feel fine, and you have a solution in your machine at least until we come up with something."

"I guess. I'm just terrified of what might happen to you."

"We can't live or think that way—in fear. We have to take hold of each day and live it to its fullest; otherwise, what's the point?"'

Dunstan sat up and looked across at her silently. The sun created a golden glow in the room, and his eyes shone like iridescent pools of light. "Desti, I feel like you are all I have in this world and the next. Can we do this? I mean, are you sure—do you want to be with me?"

"Surer than I could ever be, considering ..." She trailed off as he rose from the bed, leaving her entranced with the sight of him.

He fiddled in the drawer of the beautiful Brazilian rosewood chest of drawers and returned to her sitting on the edge of the bed. "Then my love—would you consider this?" he asked.

She didn't notice the small velvet box until he got up and knelt beside her.

"I don't know if this is crazy," he said. "I don't know how we would be able to explain it here at least. In fact, I don't know much of anything. The one thing I do know is that you were made for me and me for you. It may seem obsessive, but I've been carrying this thing around since I found you here, determined to put this on your finger the way I promised when we were younger. Now with everything that is unfolding, I know that time and life are just too precious to waste." His eyes grew wide and misty as he spoke.

He opened the box, and inside lay the most beautiful piece Desti had ever seen. It was an engagement ring featuring a rectangular yellow diamond flanked by two trapezoidal white diamonds, surrounded by other smaller diamonds. The sun caught the center diamond's yellow hue, and tiny lights reflected from the ring in the eyes now looking up at her.

"Destiny Tallum, take this journey with me. Walk with me step by step every day for the rest of our lives. Please do me the honor and say that you will marry me."

A single tear fell from Destiny's eye and seemed to be absorbed in the brilliance of the ring. She was dumbstruck. She trembled at the thought of spending whatever life she had with the man she loved, and of being with him for the rest of their lives. "Yes, Dunstan. Oh, yes, yes, yes!" she replied, without a bit of hesitation in her voice.

Tears flowed freely then from them both, and they held each other for a long time without saying a word. They had each other, and that was all that mattered. In her heart Desti vowed never to let go of this feeling, never to let go of the total trust and security she felt in Dunstan's arms; she vowed to follow him to the ends of the earth if she had to.

Dunstan kissed her tenderly and sweetly, his heart bursting at the seams. Finally, they could be together, and he too vowed that no one and nothing would separate them. It was a while before either of them spoke again.

Destiny was watching the sun creep across the room when suddenly she remembered the composition she'd written the night before. "Dunstan, I have to show you something." She crawled over him and reached for the sheets of music on the table. "I wrote this last night, and I have no idea how." She showed him the notes.

Dunstan took the pages from her and looked up at her quizzically. "Have you done this before that you can remember?" he asked.

"Not that I can remember." She went on to describe the process she'd gone through.

"Let's go hear what this sounds like," Dunstan said, heading to the bathroom to wash his face and brush his teeth. Destiny watched him walk away and pictured herself waking up every day exactly like this for the rest of her life. She could definitely get used to this, she thought, as went to join him.

A few minutes later, they were scanning her sheet music into Dunstan's computer, and soon, the notes were transformed into a melody so sweet and entrancing that the entire house seemed to reverberate with the love Destiny had felt when she penned it.

"This is fantastic – you've got to name it." Dunstan replied, selecting repeat so that they could listen once again.

"I don't know how I did this, but something is happening to me that I can't explain," she said. "My headaches are gone, and although I can't remember much of anything still, things feel familiar." She touched her chest over her heart to emphasize how she felt. "There is something else that I started thinking about while I was back in the US." She sighed and went to the mirrored panel on the wall. "I haven't aged." Destiny turned around to face him. "Over the last seven years, I don't think that I've aged. I used to think that I had really great genes, but deep down, something feels off. Do you think that this could be possible? That I haven't aged because of the jump?"

Dunstan sat and thought about it. "Desti, you may be absolutely right. I remember when I first saw you, I thought to myself how impossible it was for you to be so unbelievably beautiful, like you hadn't aged a bit in all the years." He sat up now, furrowing his brow. "But I chalked it up to my being love-struck. The more I look at you, the more I think you may be onto something. Why don't we find out for sure? Pete and Ayala can help with that. They can run some tests to see your true age."

"How? I mean, I watch CSI." Destiny laughed. "Doesn't the person have to be dead so you can analyze the skull and other bone features?"

Before Dunstan could answer, Pete came through the door and kissed his baby sister on the cheek, tapping his forehead as an indication of how he and Dunstan had communicated. Pete was ecstatic and congratulated them, almost crushing them with hugs once he spied the ring on Destiny's finger, which was in fact hard to miss in its brilliance. He kissed his sister and said, "You forget that we are a bit more advanced over there than here. I think that we can work something out, but we are going to have to take an MRI. It's time for you to see the basement of this house."

They all got up to leave, but Destiny pulled Dunstan and wrapped herself in his arms.

"I've already named this piece." She said, locking herself in his glare. "I've called it New Beginnings."

Destiny followed Dunstan to the sublevel of the house, which was otherworldly. Ayala and Pete were there, along with a few others Destiny didn't know.

"You know, when you and Pete first told me about my past, you should have just shown me down here—would have saved us a few months of torture," Destiny said with a chuckle.

"Well, that was the plan," Dunstan replied, nudging her good-naturedly, referring to her hasty exit on the day they'd tried to tell her.

A few hours later, the results came in: Destiny's body was frozen in time—her body had stopped aging the day she jumped.

The two couples were now seated at the dinner table, going over what they had discovered. Pete and Dunstan surmised that the aging process had stopped when Destiny arrived, which opened up the incredible possibility that once she jumped back, she would just age to where she should be – just as how Charm had done. Once the results had come in, they'd actually jumped a few strands of her hair. Not only did they make it over to the other side, but tests showed that the hair aged seven years—and actually regenerated and grew.

"What if I jump and I continue to age exponentially?" Destiny asked.

The table became silent. They had all thought of this, but the truth was that only time would tell.

Finally, Dunstan replied, "We should wait it out." He took her hand. "We've waited for seven years; what's some more time on this side? Let's wait it out. Let's wait and see what your cells do in a few months."

The next day, Dunstan and Destiny headed over to see Stella and Ethan. After exchanging hugs and laughter, they settled on the porch with a pot of fresh coffee. Stella held Destiny's hand, her eyes misty, as she silently watched her son totally happy and at ease.

"Well, first off, Desti and I … well, we're getting married," Dunstan said, a broad smile on his face as he spoke.

Stella and Ethan were elated, and Ethan replaced their coffee with a bottle of champagne. After they toasted, Stella became quiet and asked, "How are you going to live? Well, where are you going to live?"

"We're going back," Dunstan replied. "We don't belong here; we're going home." He sighed before continuing. "I'm not sure how. Whenever I have jumped back to our world, I've gone to sleep here. I don't know what will happen if I detach for a length of time and never return. That's why I need you to help him—the Dunstan who remains. If anything goes wrong, you need to be there for him, help him run the company, sell it—whatever you need to do so as not to raise any questions. I've already put things in place in case the worst should happen." Dunstan sighed, suddenly feeling more tired than he had in a long time.

"I can't keep jumping like this—it's taking a toll on me. I took too many risks in the early days looking for Desti. We've found a way to jump Desti back, and if we are successful, we'll need your help with her disappearance here in this dimension. We have to wait a bit longer to ensure that she will be okay on the other side. Ayala and Pete—they can keep jumping; they aren't aging as much or as quickly as I am, so the only abnormal factors will be me and Desti, but we've done as much as we can."

Ethan listened quietly as he looked at this family, which was both his and not really his. He thought back to the first time he'd met Stella and about how much his life had changed since meeting her. He couldn't help but think about how much it was all going to change again.

Chapter 21

------ ᴡᴡ-◦-ᴏᴄ⊙ᴏ⊙⊙-ᴏ-ᴡᴡ ------

I t was a cool evening when Desti and Dunstan walked down the aisle. She wore a silk strapless Mia Solano gown with a ruched bodice. A yellow band around the bodice matched her engagement ring, and the dress's chapel train was inset beautifully, detailed with silver embroidery. Ayala and Dunstan had replaced the beading with tiny diamonds as a surprise. "I look like I'm glowing," she said quietly when she looked at herself in the mirror, as the tiny diamonds picked up the yellow light of the evening sun filtering into the room. She felt a pang of sadness as she wished that her parents were there with her. She longed for the comfort of a mom who would come and fuss over her unnecessarily or a sister who would straighten her dress and tell her she was going to blow her groom away. Pete came in then and held his sister at arm's length for fear of crushing her dress. In spite of his attempt to be cautious, Destiny hugged him fiercely.

"Thank you, Pete. Thank you for never giving up on me," Destiny said, racked with emotion.

Before the tears could come, Pete painted a scene in her head of them and their dad watching the setting sun on what would be his last birthday. Their dad had said to them that the ultimate happiness for him would be to see them grown and having found the same kind of love that he and their mom had shared, a love that would take them through every possible situation, built on honesty, respect, and trust. *"You've got that with Dunstan,"* Pete said. *"You've made Dad's wish come true. We both have."*

Just then, Ayala and Stella bustled in and paused at the door as Destiny spun for them.

"Why, Desti, you are absolutely gorgeous!" Stella said, coming to her side. "Here, let me fix these pins for you." Stella gently took her by the arm and led her to the chair in front of the dressing area. She carefully reset the pins in Destiny's hair and touched up her face.

Destiny's eyes moistened, and she reached up to pull Stella's arm around her. They held each other for a few seconds, and with misty eyes, Destiny said, "Thank you, Stella, for everything that you've done for us."

"Oh, sweetie, I'm so glad that he has you," Stella said, hugging her tighter.

Ayala bustled over and shooed Stella away. "Now, now, none of this—we can't have her ruining her makeup or yours. She has a groom outside itching to see her – I swear he will leave track marks in the grass if he doesn't stop pacing up and down! This is a happy day—no tears!" She laughed, wiping some of her own. It was then that Destiny realized that she did indeed have the family that she'd been longing for earlier.

Destiny hadn't wanted to unnecessarily expend the energy of the small group around her with the details of a fussy wedding, and although Dunstan had agreed in concept, he had convinced her that this was easily going to be one of the most memorable events of their lives—and since they (or he) could afford it, no expense would be spared, even if it was a small wedding.

Thus, the gardens at Dunstan's home in Italy had been transformed into a fairy-tale scene. White silk draped each of twelve columns sectioning off the wedding area, and the huge outdoor tent was decorated with tiny chandeliers and roses. Each table was beautifully set with ice sculptures as centerpieces, with each setting placed on glass trays. Tiny lights bounced off of every reflective piece, making the entire garden shine and gleam; it felt almost ethereal.

As Destiny walked down the path, she looked around at the people who were now a part of her existence and wondered for a brief moment what future she would have. Any pangs of fear or wonder dissipated immediately when Dunstan turned to face her. His lower jaw dropped slightly at the sight of her, and every emotion that he felt was transparent on his face. Pete, who had unfortunately had to choose between walking his sister down the aisle and being his best friend's best man, lit up as he watched the two, and Destiny was sure that it was because he was capturing a memory.

When Destiny reached Dunstan's side, he took her hand and kissed her on the cheek, gently and sweetly. "You look amazing, Desti. I can't believe how lucky I am," he said softly.

Destiny was too choked up to speak; all she could do was nod her head so that the tears she knew were coming would hold back a little while longer. Dunstan and Destiny had opted to write their own vows, and there wasn't a dry eye under the setting Tuscan sun as they recited them to each other.

"Destiny, you have given me the meaning of existence. Living without you is not an option because being with you is all that I know. Your grace, elegance, beauty, and intelligence make you perfect in my eyes. When I'm away from you, thoughts of your smile caress my mind, and I never feel far away because you are forever with me in my heart. I promise to love and honor you, grow with you, grow old with you, protect and cherish you, be the man and husband that you deserve. You are my air, and I will live and breathe you forever." Dunstan wiped the tears away from Destiny's eyes as he placed the wedding band on her hand.

"Dunstan, from the very first time I heard your sweet voice, I knew you'd be my choice. Being near you makes me feel so full inside; it's the simple things about you that drive me wild. It's the touch of your hand on the side of my face, the depth in your eyes, a memory I can't erase. A memory so true, an angel's heart is in you; you are my gift sent from heaven; you are my dream come true. Roses on my pillow are your words in my brain; your laughter and your love, they keep me sane. I promise to love and respect you, grow old with you through thick and thin, and be your support, your lover, and your friend." Now it was Destiny's turn to wipe the tear falling down Dunstan's cheek as she placed his ring on his finger.

"Her vows trumped yours, for sure!" Pete said, sending thoughts their way. Neither Dunstan nor Destiny could help but laugh out loud, despite the confusion the sudden outburst must have caused the small gathering of friends who had been invited to witness the ceremony.

As she walked back down the small pathway with her hand tucked under Dunstan's arm, Destiny stopped to hug Ethan and Stella. She winked at Roth and Anna, who she now knew were also from Dunstan's dimension and had been watching over her from the day she joined their team. Vera had declined the invitation politely, and Destiny had heard that she was beside herself from the day that she found out that Destiny and Dunstan had become engaged. The other guests included the Italian directors whom Destiny had met with back in the train and a few other business colleagues who were oblivious to anything other than what they were presented with.

While Destiny and Dunstan were in the middle of their first dance to Destiny's composition "Gray Skies," an older man approached and tapped Dunstan lightly on his shoulder. Destiny thought he looked like an older version of her new husband.

"Mind if I ask my new daughter for this dance?" the man asked.

Dunstan turned and exclaimed, "Dad!" Dunstan embraced his father and said softly, "I can't believe it—that you actually jumped to be here." As Dunstan stood next to his father, he overshadowed him by only a few inches. They shared the same piercing gray eyes and dark hair.

"I couldn't miss my only son's big day now, could I?" Dunstan's dad replied, clapping him lightly on the back.

"This means so much to me. I know how hard it must be for you to be here," Dunstan said, looking in Ethan and Stella's direction.

Dunstan's father merely smiled and seemed to intentionally focus his attention and effort on the couple before him.

"Dad, here she is—Destiny," Dunstan said, pulling Destiny gently from behind him.

"Destiny. Darius Moab. At last we meet again. You are just as pretty now as you were then. I understand why Dunstan was so persistent in finding you." Destiny extended her hand, but Dunstan's dad embraced her instead, whispering in her ear, "Welcome to the family, and hopefully soon we will be having this conversation on the other side."

The rest of the evening continued to be perfect, though Destiny noticed that Dunstan's dad stayed as far as he could from Stella and Ethan before eventually bidding the newlyweds farewell, long before the evening's festivities were over. As the couple milled through the small gathering, Destiny noticed Stella move off to one side of the garden on her own, dabbing her eyes. Destiny went over to join her.

"Need some company?" Destiny asked, sitting on the stone bench beside her.

Stella shook her head and feigned a smile. "What are you doing here away from your new husband? Go, I just need a breather."

But Destiny could see how hard Stella was fighting to hold back the tears. She took Stella's hand and said to her softly, "I can't imagine what you and Dunstan's dad are going through. A vow never to communicate again? I know that you are still mad about him. I can see it all over you."

Stella exhaled deeply and slowly. "It's still that obvious, isn't it? Oh my, what must Ethan be thinking?"

They both remained quiet for a few seconds. "Stella, you know that I love Ethan like family. He is the only father-like figure I have in my life. I would never do or say anything to hurt him in any way. But to live like this … there must be another way. They have the rejuvenation chamber now. Maybe Dunstan's dad can jump back and forth so that the two of you can be together. I finally know what it is to love—I mean, the kind of love that can never be extinguished, not by time, space, or circumstance. I think that's what you have for Dunstan's dad. Sometimes you need to be selfish and think about what you need. What makes you happy?"

"I could never really be happy knowing that I've hurt someone as sweet and as loving as Ethan, no matter the circumstance. He's been there for me through thick and thin. I will never forget that," Stella replied. "Darius and I made a pact—no contact ever again so that we could move on with our lives."

"Doesn't look to me like either of you have moved on," Destiny replied.

In the shadows, Destiny barely spotted Ethan as he turned away from them, and she chose not to tell Stella that perhaps he had overheard their conversation. The two women rejoined the guests a few minutes later. Destiny saw that Stella had done an amazing job at composing herself well enough that no one else could tell how upset she was, though she could see a change in Ethan from the moment he took Stella's hand and guided her back to the table where he was seated. He had a faraway look in his eyes, and Destiny's heart filled with empathy at their situation.

Pete was about to give his best-man speech, and Dunstan and Destiny looked forward to the cheerful banter that was sure to ensue. Pete was true to his reputation, and everyone was in stitches by the time he was done. At the end of his speech, Pete asked Ayala to stand next to him to raise a toast to his family.

Chapter 22

It was a perfect day to end her life here. As the yacht sailed toward the Greek isle of Kefalonia, the smell of leaking gasoline was pungent. The captain of the vessel searched for the leak and radioed for help. The smell of burning wood from below, where Dunstan and Desti lay resting, set off alarms.

The captain quickly gave the abandon-ship order and briefly saw Dunstan and Desti emerge from the quarters below, their faces covered as they tried to escape from the smoke. They disappeared around the side of the boat, where the lifeboats lay stacked. The captain tried to advance toward them, but the smoke was too thick, and the flames licked at his arms. He could hear the wail of a Greek coast guard ship, which he had radioed, but it was still a distance away. He looked out and saw that two lifeboats were already in the water; assured that everyone else had made it off first, the captain grabbed his life jacket and hurled himself off of the ship. He had barely hit the surface when a loud explosion echoed against the rising tide. He swallowed water but was able to resurface and saw both boats moving farther away, safely away from the inferno.

The coast guard reached him first and threw over a life rope for him; as he pulled himself over the side, he was shivering but happy to be alive. The ship was headed toward the flashing beacon of the other lifeboats when the sky suddenly lit up. A piece of the mast had jettisoned into the air and was now on its way back down—and to the captain's disbelief and horror, it was plummeting straight toward one of the small crafts bobbing in the ocean. Everyone began yelling at once, and the captain of the coast guard vessel increased the pace of the ship, to try to block the path of the burning piece of wood.

"No, no, no!" the captain murmured as the piece of wood speared the lifeboat easily, tearing it in two. He watched as two bodies ejected from the boat.

Destiny opened her eyes and looked around. Dunstan looked down on her, eyes bright and wet. She was a little confused at first, but soon everything came back to her in a flash. Everything around her felt different. The air seemed to buzz with an energy that she couldn't explain. The air felt fresher, cleaner, and different. She slowly looked around from face to face at everyone in the room. Pete and Ayala were there, and of course so was her one true love, Dunstan. Two men dressed in white were removing electrodes from her temples and running tiny handheld devices up and down her body. She heard an electronic pulse that kept pace with her heart. She sat up slowly and smiled brightly at everyone looking at her.

"*Did we do it?*" she asked silently.

"*We sure did!*" Dunstan and Pete answered in unison.

Ayala came closer to her and asked, "Are you okay? How do you feel?"

"I feel different—absolutely wonderful, but different." Destiny sat up and reached out to both Dunstan and Pete. She wanted to see everything around her, to make sure that everything was real and indeed happening right now. Dunstan took her hand and kissed her forehead gently. He reached into his pocket and placed a new wedding band on her finger to replace the one that she'd had to leave behind.

Destiny smiled and kissed his neck and cheek. She then turned to Pete, who was looking at his little sister with an expression full of emotion, as if his heart was bursting at the seams.

Dunstan moved a strand of her hair behind her ear and helped her up. "We did it, my love—you're here. Welcome home, my sweet love," he said. The love flowing between them seemed to envelop the room.

Destiny inhaled sharply and looked around, her eye sparkling. "Guys, you know what else?"

They all looked at her quizzically.

"I remember. I remember everything."

Epilogue

It had been three months since the accident, and he was no closer to remembering what had happened. In fact, the last few years of his life were a blur. He had a company to run, and he had no idea what he needed to do. He had checked himself into the best treatment facility he could find and had spent days trying to force himself to remember pieces of his life that were just missing. He could not bring himself to grieve for a wife he had lost in the same accident because he simply couldn't remember who she was, and her body hadn't been found.

Despite his situation, however, he felt content with his lot, as if his life was complete and he had accomplished all that he could. He rotated his shoulder, which he had used to block the blow of the falling timber, or so he'd been told. It was practically healed now. He inhaled the salty Hawaiian air and resigned himself to the doctor's prognosis—that the severity of the injury he'd sustained meant that he might never regain his full memory. He paddled out and sat waiting for the next wave to fall in. It was then that he saw her. She was the most beautiful person he had ever laid eyes on. Her hair was slick from the waves, which accentuated her beauty, and she commanded the wave like a symphony. He couldn't help himself—he swam as fast as he could to meet her as she headed toward the shore.

She glanced over her shoulder, and their eyes met. Instantly, they held each other's gaze, as if they had been caught in this trance before. A smile formed on her lips as a crashing wave arrived and wiped him out. She half-swam, half-paddled to his side and helped him to shore. They fell to the sand, both laughing at what had just happened.

"I know this may sound cheesy, but have we met before?" he asked.

"No, I don't think so," she replied. "I think that I would have remembered those eyes." She outstretched her hand and smiled. "My name is Destiny," she said. As Destiny shook the water from her hair, the chain around her neck clinked with its pendant, which was engraved "D&D" intertwined around a rose.

He cocked his head to the side as something clicked in his brain. He took her outstretched hand and replied, "Dunstan."